DECOMMISSIONED CHINA

CHINA

退役的中国

MARYELLEN HUNTER

Copyright © 2020 Maryellen Hunter

All rights reserved.

ISBN: 978-1-7358448-5-5 (paperback)
ISBN: 978-1-7358448-4-8 (ebook)

DEDICATION

For my Maestro of Munitions

THANK YOU

To Bob for his technical contributions and for suffering through the editing process again and again.

To Brenda S for being my Facebook sister!

PROLOG

The United States begins to recover from the genocide perpetrated by a small group of oligarchs with their masterplan of Clearcutting a targeted portion of the population deemed a burden on the economy and a threat to their power. The small group was a collection of politicians and bureaucrats – referred to as the DComm Group because their viral method of genocide was identified in their mission statement as Decommissioning.

The DComm Group was discovered by a small collection of patriots calling themselves the Savior Unit. Savior managed to expose the criminal act being perpetrated upon the population, of the United States, but the loss of over 12 million citizens had occurred before the truth was known and the people revolted to take back control of the country.

Now, three key members of the DComm Group are up to something in China, the details of which are not yet fully known. The Savior Unit's mission has not ended as these DComm Group members must be found and stopped. It's up to key members of the Savior Unit and their contacts in China to; uncover the details of a plot against the Chinese people, hunt down these vile perpetrators and bring them to justice.

STEPHANIE
IN FLIGHT

Stephanie Wolff, former Director of the United States National Security Administration (NSA) is now aboard one of her private jets with Chuck Delphi, former Director of United States Department of Defense (DOD) on their way to Beijing, China. Her plane is loaded with approximately 30,000 units, divided into equal parts, of JMV2030 (raw virus), JMV2030_R (randomized bio-weapon), and AV_JMV2030 (anti-virus to the bio-weapon). Her other plane contained more of the virus and vaccine, but it had disappeared somewhere over the South Pacific, near New Zealand. Her pilot was instructed not to report the missing plane, due to the lethal cargo.

Unfortunately, the other plane went down with another of her pilots, but Stephanie is not prone to matters of guilt or remorse. She has the raw virus and that is most important. From that, there will be ample opportunities to grow more of the serums. She thinks to herself, *it is unfortunate that Chuck Delphi decided to invite himself to ride in my plane, the man is obnoxious, a loudmouth, and a liability unsurpassed by none, in addition to being an insatiable sexual predator, more*

1

loathsome than a cockroach. Soon I am going to make arrangements to have him decommissioned - in China.

Once she gets to Beijing, she will be able to obtain a secure line to Vice President Hoge and Darla Avery (CIA) to advise them of the inventory loss. She won't suggest decommissioning Delphi - yet. There could be some temporary need for him to reestablish the DComm Group and coordinate plans for the Chinese Clearcut process. She does not know that before the end of the week, Art Damone will be arriving in Beijing.

BEIJING HVD MEETING

Upon landing in Beijing, Stephanie was met by a representative of Dr. Yīshēng to take her and Chuck to a meeting at the Beijing Ministries' offices. It had been a seventeen-hour flight during which her only respite from the scotch influenced ranting of Chuck Delphi was her pretense at sleeping. After a few hours of being ignored and drinking, he finally shut his foul mouth and she was able to take a real nap. She wasn't fresh as a daisy, but she wasn't hungover.

In attendance:
Stephanie Wolff (Former USA NSA)
Chuck Delphi (Former USA DOD)
Dr. Yīshēng Sǐwáng (Former Director Bearlywoke Storage - USA)
Darla Avery (Director USA CIA - tele-video)
Robert Hoge (Vice President USA - tele-video)

Stephanie assumed the role of leadership in the meeting, it was just her nature to do so. "In attendance today we have Chuck Delphi, Doctor Yīshēng of Beijing China,

Darla Avery, Vice President Robert Hoge, and myself, Stephanie Wolff. I will attempt to abbreviate the meeting today. Doctor Yīshēng, can you please give us a status update on the virus production and research?"

Dr. Yīshēng, "Yes, the original JMV2030 and its anti-virus are being manufactured with great efficiency. Based on their improved growth patterns, we are packaging approximately 50,000 units per day now. I have been shipping supplies here for months before the initial launch of USA Project Clearcut, so in addition to the JMV manufacturing process, my scientists have been working on a synthetic version of the vaccines. A synthetic will be produced faster than growing live cultures and can be packaged in a tablet or capsule form to allow for export at a lower cost per unit."

Darla, "It is my understanding that there was a store of active virus aboard the now missing plane. Does anyone have any information about the missing plane?"

Stephanie, "Nothing at all. The only way someone would be looking would be if it was on the radar when it disappeared. I don't believe we were in the radar range of New Zealand when it went down. My pilot received no emergency call from them, so if the damn thing sunk, I hope it is deep. What's the bounty on us now, Darla?"

Darla, "Hmmm, Chuck is at three million, yours is one million."

Delphi, "Well there you go Stephanie – see what you've been missing all this time? I keep telling you we are on the same team and it could be pretty comfy if we spent more time together."

Stephanie, "Shut your perverted mouth Chuck, if I had my way you would have been in the deep blue sea with that jet!"

Darla, in a loud voice, "Stop you two! Doctor Yīshēng, can you give me an estimate of when China is going to start dispensing the Chinese version of HVD? Vice President

Hoge and I would like to know because he will need to pull journalists out of the country before you launch. We can't afford to have the USA citizens begin another uprising if they get scared from seeing HVD killing over there."

Dr. Yīshēng, "We are about to launch in the political prisons and re-education camps. These are very secure locations and there is no risk of video or stories leaking out of those places. The Chinese Ministry of Communication is the very best in the world at preventing the escape of information to and from our shores. Our media people are preparing the video reports to frighten our people and drive them to get vaccinated as we did in the USA. Television here is state-run, so there will be nothing viewed that we don't approve of, assuming that you get the U.S. journalists removed.

We have been translating the propaganda videotapes from English to Chinese and other Asian languages, so these videos of dying USA citizens will bring the Asians to get vaccinated. We will mix videos of the dying in the camps without showing the locations to ensure that our country believes that the HVD has become pandemic."

Vice President Hoge, "Thank you Doctor. Again, I would respectfully request that you provide specific dates for the shipments of Chinese prepared HVD products to be distributed with the planned destinations. We will need to know your timeline to ensure that our media is properly instructed and in sync with that of your state-run broadcasts. This information may be transmitted to Director Avery, to be shared with me. My position within the administration keeps me surrounded with the potential for media leaks, so secure transmission of data would be better conveyed through her. If there are no questions for us, we will leave you to your meeting, and look forward to the requested data."

There were no questions, so Vice President Hoge and Darla disconnected assuming that his request would be complied with. They could care less about how the doctor planned to deploy the HVD to his own country. Their only concern was ensuring that the U.S. citizens didn't see bad media reports of China and react against the United States government.

The meeting continued with Stephanie's attention turning to the Doctor. "Doctor Yīshēng, I'd like to ask for more information about your HVD distribution and target planning, but it's been a pretty long trip for us and I would appreciate having a meeting after I've had a few days to recover from the jet lag."

Chuck chimed in, "Doctor, can you tell me where I might find some 'female companionship' to occupy my time while we wait on the launch?"

Stephanie sat quietly, rolled her eyes, and shook her head slightly at the brazen request.

Dr. Yīshēng, with a sly smile, responded, "Ahhh, yes Mr. Delphi, your personal appetite for the ladies precedes you. I will send you some visitors this evening, they speak English and will do as they are instructed. Enjoy your time in China, Mr. Delphi. Miss Wolff, may I indulge you to stay a few minutes longer?"

Chuck departed the meeting quickly as he already anticipated the prospect of indulging in some Asian flesh. Once Chuck had left, Dr. Yīshēng addressed Stephanie, "Miss Wolff, at the risk of being indelicate, I would ask you if there is anything I can provide to make your time here in China more interesting or entertaining? I mean no disrespect when I say that you are a very beautiful woman and will surely draw attention no matter where you go.

I might suggest that I could provide your choice of escorts to protect you in this unfamiliar city. This would be for your protection of course and a means to pass some time experiencing our culture and entertainment. I could send gentlemen or ladies for you to choose what would best suit your interests. Even a lady going on shopping trips might choose a gentleman for protection but a lady for shopping. Here is my card with my cell phone number on it. I would be honored to send a few people who are familiar with our city and culture. If they are not acceptable, you can call me and I will send others until you find acceptable companions. As I said, I mean this in no disrespect, if you have no desire to avail yourself of such services, I will leave that to you."

Stephanie, "Thank you for your discretion Doctor. I will be pleased to accept your kind offer and look forward to interviewing whomever you send. Will 8 PM be a good time this evening? Of course, I will wish to shop in the morning but the possibility of discovering this unique city will please me very much."

CHAIRMAN ZHÁNG WEI JUN
AND
DR. YĪSHĒNG SǏWÁNG

Dr. Yīshēng, "Honorable Mr. Chairman, I have just met with the Americans for a status on the virus production, they are pleased with the volume of material we are producing. Our scientists are making slight modifications to the dissemination methods of the virus including ingestion in addition to aerial and injection. This is not information shared with the Americans.

I did not mention that we have people working on the testing phase of the GMO modified rice. The Americans foolishly believe that this virus is intended for the clearcutting of Asians only. They believe that they are assisting China in ridding itself of the young revolutionaries with their dreams of democracy and insurrection against the supreme commander's control of our blessed country.

At this time, it seems that we have little use for the Americans. Since their country has no idea where they are, perhaps you would wish me to make arrangements for their disposal?"

Chairman Zháng, "You have done well Doctor Yīshēng, leave the Americans to their fantasies for now. Perhaps they need to indulge in something addictive to take their minds off their mission. Mr. Delphi imagines himself to be a ladies' man, so he should be easy enough to control. I'm told that Miss Wolff likes men who like to be controlled. Do you think you can see to the accommodations of her particular taste? Have you considered the possibility of introducing them to some of our very special addictive pharmaceuticals?"

Dr. Yīshēng, "I have a variety of comfort escorts in mind to service their unique tastes and have made the arrangements. Ms. Wolff was accommodating and receptive to my offer as well. However, I had not considered the variety of pharmaceuticals we have at our disposal. Thank you sir, for the most excellent suggestion.

My staff informs me that the bounty on their heads continues to rise. I have people searching for the missing plane. Perhaps if the plane is found, it could be a means to raise the price on their heads even more."

Chairman Zháng, "I will tell you an ancient story, Doctor. Once upon a time, there was an old farmer planting acres of crops. Every day he went to the field to watch the crops grow. He noticed the seedlings growing little by little each day. He thought they were growing too slowly and got impatient with the young plants. 'How could the plants grow faster?' he thought. Bothered by this question, he could not fall asleep. Suddenly he happened upon an idea which he could not wait to practice.

He jumped from the bed and rushed to the field immediately. One by one, he pulled up the seedlings by half again their height under the moonlight. He did not finish pulling until the next morning. Straightening his back, he said to himself, 'What a wonderful idea! Look, how much taller the plants have grown in one night!' With great satisfaction, he went back home. He told his son what he had done in a triumphant tone. His son was shocked. Now the sun had risen. The young man was heart-broken to see all the pulled-up young plants dying.

So, let us not be like the farmer in this story I have just shared with you, to make haste by clearing the garden of these Americans. Let us instead be patient as they have proven to be useful tools. We have no shortage of money, my friend, what we seek is the power for which we have waited generations to execute.

Please let me know when we will be ready to begin exporting the new Clearcut Rice. And I would also like to know when you are ready for me to put my military to dispensing the virus inside the political re-education camps."

Dr. Yīshēng, "Ahhh, Chairman, I see we think from one mind, but that you are infinitely wiser. I had not considered that the Americans would be of further value. I will see that they are comfortably detained and ensure that the 'escorts' are equipped with sufficient pharmaceuticals."

Immediately after departing, the Doctor placed several calls with instructions to report to him daily the results of the encounters. He wanted to know what type of interest these two Americans had. It wouldn't take long to discover their tastes and the value of the videotaped entertainment they would be indulging in with their comfort escorts. He thought, *There is no such thing as too much information when you are dealing with the enemies of the state.*

RE-EDUCATION CAMPS

Dr. Yīshēng's scientists had not been idle. In his Dongguan laboratory they had created, for purposes of use in the re-education camps, a liquid synthetic serum to be added to food and beverage to clear the camps. The camps needed to be evacuated to make way for future needs. These political and ethnic detainees were currently overcrowded and costing more to the state than could be recovered by the slave labor they provided. The Asian DComm Group was escalating their plans to be rid of all possible revolutionaries around the globe.

Chairman Zháng only needed to issue the order to initiate the clearing of these facilities as 'reeducation' was a ruse. The political prisoners were no more than slaves until they were spent then they were re-purposed. They had been using the dead bodies to feed those remaining within the camps for years.

In a meeting, the next day, Chairman Zháng sought a solution from the good Doctor, "Doctor Yīshēng, we have many things to discuss – I have these Hong Kong youths that bear a wish for democracy, and they desire to upset the regime with their foolish dreams to live like the Americans on streets paved in gold. Our military has been unsuccessful in containing them and our re-education camps are full. So honor me, if you will Doctor, with the good news of solutions to turn the foolish ones from their destruction."

Dr. Yīshēng, "Most Honorable Chairman, my laboratory facility has many people working to provide quantities of the serum which will be added to the food of the desolate ones in the camps. We are now prepared with sufficient quantities to begin. As soon as you give the order, I will see to the delivery of this material to the camps. Perhaps the upcoming New Year is an opportunity to serve them special meals containing the HVD serum. Have your military personnel prepared sufficient areas for the mass graves, or is it your plan to process the bodies to feed the incoming foolish ones?"

Chairman Zháng, "The pits are being dug. There will be sufficient fresh food from the demise of the incoming foolish ones. I believe the cost of processing and storage is a deficit when considering the lower cost of the synthetic HVD. But again, what are we doing to compel the foolish ones in the streets to be treated to the virus?"

Dr. Yīshēng, "We have videos running, images of the dying Americans, with warnings that the Americans have brought this deadly destruction to our beloved red state to kill China without the use of military action. These videos bring the families to the medical facilities to get injected.

The foolish freedom marchers, however, refuse the vaccines because of the propaganda from the United States claiming the virus inoculations were false. I have taken the action of having the serum introduced to a water bottling production to provide free bottles of water to the foolish ones as they parade in the streets with no mission in life other than themselves."

Chairman Zháng, "Ah Doctor, this is well considered. Give the democracy seekers free things – like in America. You must do this, immediately."

Dr. Yīshēng, "Yes Chairman, I already took this action of preparing an existing bottling plant. The addition of the serum goes into bottles labeled Freedom!! These bottles appear to come as support from the Americans."

Chairman Zháng, "Doctor, you are wise beyond your status but do not allow your ambition to reach beyond your station. I'm sure you meant no disrespect in taking such an action without advising me. Perhaps you mentioned this to me and it slipped my mind."

Dr. Yīshēng, "Honorable Chairman, you have my loyalty. I am certain that some foolish administrator neglected to remind you of our conversation about this action."

Chairman Zháng, "And what are we to do with the Americans, Doctor, when the time is right to clear the garden?"

Dr. Yīshēng, "Rice, honorable Chairman."

Chairman Zháng, "Rice?"

Dr. Yīshēng, "America imports more than 20% of the rice grown in China. The Honorable Chairman can send an offer of an attractively priced trade agreement for the special rice. This would restart the reduction of the United States population with no plans for targeted groups. The **laowai** (*Chinese derogatory slang for foreigners*) will not be vaccinated to our new modified strain of HVD, but there was much destruction and loss during the rioting process, their food supplies will not be recovered until the next harvest time. Our offer of the specially-priced rice should be easily accepted."

Dr. Yīshēng, wisely, did not mention that he had taken the initiative to have the GMO rice grown and harvested, or that it was already being used in the manufacture of the Freedom Power Bars in addition to bags for export to the USA. The Chairman was old and he had dreams of holding the world in his palm, but the doctor knew that dreams are not fulfilled without action. The doctor was not a dreamer,

15

he was an innovator, and the Chairman would soon outlive his usefulness in the New World Order.

Chairman Zháng, "Then I believe that you must return to Dongguan once you have made the arrangements for the American's entertainment. You have reliable agents to monitor and control these events in Beijing?"

Dr. Yīshēng needed only to bow humbly and back out of the presence of his commander. He had a few delegation tasks to perform before he flew back to Dongguan.

***

The USA

Vice President Hoge called the Secretary of State to share that the CIA had reliable intelligence indicating there were some very bad things about to happen with regards to the Freedom Fighters in China and it was best to recall all American ambassadors and media people from that country. The Vice President did not know that this information was false. He was under the misimpression that his relationship with the DComm Project Clearcut extended to the Chinese version of the operation. He did not know that the Chinese State propaganda would be blaming the USA for the epidemic about to befall China.

***

China Media Blitz

The single state-controlled media was now running video loops showing images of Americans sick and dying in hospital beds and on streets – young and old, male and female. Images included rioting within the lines of United States citizens fighting to get their vaccinations.

请安排您的拍摄时间，不要让这种情况在中国发生
(CALL TO SCHEDULE YOUR SHOT, DO NOT LET THIS HAPPEN IN CHINA)

今天打电话
(CALL TODAY)

Other videos looped in with those from the USA. There were videos of dead and dying inside the political re-education camps. Of course, these videos were taken cautiously to ensure that the locations were not as recognizable as being taken in the camps within China. Political residents never returned from these 'camps'. Their presence was known but never spoken of publicly.

The Chinese equivalent of the NSA, who thought themselves superior to any such agency in the world, had facial recognition programs. All resident citizens, in the country of China, were cataloged. Their political, financial, and health information could not escape the aggregate collection inside the governmental Ministry of Security.

Stephanie Wolff had been working remotely with her Chinese counterparts as they developed the programs which would coordinate the lists of people who would be receiving the HVD and which would receive the actual anti-virus. This program was the American NSA program combined with a contact tracer that China already had operational.

The military bases across the country were already staffed with computer operators to quickly ascertain, via biometric scans, which vaccine needed to be administered by the army of sufficiently trained distributors of the vaccines.

Each inoculation center, with their scanners, directed the recipients to a line 'A' or 'B'. The biometric scanners ensured accurate identification and assignment to a specific line to receive the vaccine. The foolish freedom marchers did not get into lines for their vaccinations, but many other citizens rushed to get theirs.

ART DAMONE
IN CHINA

Art Damone, a private black ops contractor and Savior Unit member, had a reputation for being fast and efficient in the performance of his missions and in his ability to accomplish seemingly impossible tasks. He was well known to the people who could afford to pay his fee for the discreet dispatch of a political or high profile adversary.

His most recent projects, directed by the USA DOD, had been the elimination of Dr. Hampton, a high profile virologist involved in the development of the virus, Terry Angel - assistant director to a DOD manufacturing facility, Roger Ackinsen – acting director of the DOD, and Sandra H. Talbot - the sitting President of United States!

Unfortunately, the patriotic motives for his acceptance of these missions had been based on falsely represented information indicating that the jobs were necessary to the security and protection of the United States. He would never have accepted the contracts if he had known they were intended to harm his country. He was first and foremost a passionate patriot. Was he an efficient killer? Yes – but a killer with an unsurpassed moral character when it came to his loyalty to his country!

His reason for this trip to China is atonement for what he'd done in the United States. The DOD handler had deceived him, knowing exactly which buttons to push to effect Art's compliance in the killings. Killings - that violated Art's commitment to supporting the national security of his country. Killings - that took innocent lives and allowed for the genocide of the American people – people he fought to protect. And, he isn't in China for the bounties on Chuck Delphi or Stephanie Wolff.

Art's goal is to decommission the DComm Group triad of Chuck, Stephanie, and Dr. Yīshēng, now in Beijing, China. This group is preparing to execute a plan to continue the viral genocide in Asia and pave the path to make China the world power. Art knows, in his mind, that he will triumph over the evil that attempted to destroy the country of his birth, the country he has fought to save, and the country for which he is willing to die. Art's mission is not one seeking power, but rather, one fueled with the passion of patriotism. Their deaths will be his penance for the mistake of believing the false narratives provided before he had agreed to assassinate Dr. Hampton and Terry Angel and enable the DComm Group.

He has a cover, having worked in China on several occasions in the past, and is multi-lingual, but the Chinese language has many dialects. He's also going to need to tap into the Chinese communications networks. For those reasons, the Savior Unit approved the MSA, Goose, to travel with him. Goose has tools – it has sophisticated communications linking capabilities and it was programmed, before departing the United States, with a complete international language capability. Goose will ensure that there are no miscommunications while he searches for Chuck Delphi, Stephanie Wolff, and Dr. Yīshēng.

Goose had also been programmed to protect and serve

Art in the unlikely event that he gets into a situation involving self-defense that he isn't able to handle. The enhanced abilities of the droid partner might be very handy when it came time to intercept Delphi.

Art had neglected to check if there was a bounty on Dr. Yīshēng. The doctor was not a U.S. citizen, but his involvement in the U.S. DOD Project Clearcut should have qualified him as a terrorist on United States soil. Art thinks, *Quit thinking about bounties, it's not about the bounties. I got plenty of money. It's more personal. But, since Goose has my back it's more like, OUR patriotic duty.*

Chuck Delphi's secretary, Gracie Valentine, had provided some recorded conversations from Delphi to someone at Bearlywoke. And the other voice was confirmed to be the same voice that ordered Art to murder Terry Angel - none other than the voice of Dr. Yīshēng. *Yes,* he thinks, *Doctor Yīshēng is going to pay for his involvement in my killing Terry and the HVD stuff - bounty or no bounty. It's a plus that Goose was never seen by Stephanie or Dr. Yīshēng and he's got images of all three targets. Gonna be good to have him along.*

Art has been keeping in constant communications with Joshua Klein back in Texas and other members of the Savior Unit in the U.S. Goose has been communicating with other MSA's in Beijing. By the time they landed in China, Goose had the addresses of the facility that was manufacturing the HVD. When Goose shared this information Art knew he had an additional mission.

He must kill Chuck Delphi, Stephanie Wolff, and Dr. Yīshēng. But now it appears that Dr. Yīshēng has a lab making the virus to kill the Chinese. Well, some of the material Joshua had discovered from deleted computer files indicated that there was an Asia Clearcut plan – similar to the USA one. Art isn't surprised to see the Chinese government doing something like this, they had a reputation for decommissioning people who failed to agree with their goals and methods. He'd like to clear cut their

government or at least clear out the noxious parts of it –
starting with Dr. Yīshēng.

They hadn't been very long in China before they saw the
media reports indicating that HVD was in use there in
Beijing. But when he saw the 'Freedom' water bottles and
'Freedom' power bars, he was curious enough to look twice
and spot the USA flag and "Made in the USA" on the
bottles and packaging.

He asked Goose to check and see if these items were
indeed bottled and or packaged in the USA. Alarm bells
went off in Art's head, *Why would someone put labels on products
falsely representing them as coming from the United States?* Goose
had checked with Joshua and Beth back in Texas and
neither of them returned anything by that name. He noted
the items were being distributed for free to the rioters from
trucks containing Chinese words on them: "从美国免费"

Goose translated, "`Free. From the kindness of
American Democracy.`"

Art called Joanna, even though it was the middle of the
night in Texas. "I'm sorry Joanna, for calling you so late but
we have a concern that is going to need RiverMoore
evaluation. What we've discovered are three things that
seem suspicious. The Chinese are distributing truckloads of
bottled water and power bars – labeled Freedom – to the
protestors here."

Joanna, "Okay, please go on, I suspect there is a 'but'
here…"

Art, "BUT, these items are labeled 'Made in the USA'."

Joanna, "There's an AND coming isn't there?"

Art, "AND, Goose's research indicates that there is no
such company doing this distribution in America. We also
found another distribution center that is doing the
manufacturing here in China. This plant is also packaging
Freedom power bars, labeled as thank-you items to the
Americans for supporting the Chinese freedom fighters. It
is looking like the 'thank you' items are packaged for export

to the U.S. You know I'm no scientist, but Goose and I think these things need to be tested Tout de suite."

Joanna, "Art, your French is showing. Protect yourself before, during, and after obtaining the items, and do not let the items touch any article of clothing that you aren't prepared to burn. It might be safest to let Goose handle the items to ensure your safety. Can you find a vacuum bag sealing unit there? If you can, have Goose handle the items until you have them vacuum sealed and packaged for shipping. Once that is done, you can wear rubber gloves and decontaminate Goose with 91% isopropyl alcohol. It evaporates quickly and won't do any harm to his components."

Art, "Ok Joanna, we are off to do this job." He glanced at Goose then continued, "Art has tools. It's midday here, so I'm pretty sure I can get the things and get this stuff shipped off to you within the hour. I hope that we are wrong in sounding the alarm on this, but we just couldn't roll the dice knowing that Dr. Yīshēng, Delphi, and Wolff are here."

Joanna preparing to hang up said, "I'm leaving now to prepare the lab for the arrival. Please send me a message as soon as the package is on its way and exercise the most caution you've ever employed."

Just 30 minutes later Goose instant messaged her, `"Overnight Samples for evaluation - safe tools Deception - label`

Webster: Deception: something that deceives

`Must save mankind. Must save Joshua"`

All things considered, Art decided that they needed to stay as far away as possible from any protesting activity. Art paid for a single night lodging where he would first decontaminate Goose, then himself, before moving to their hotel. There was no sense to carry possible bacteria to the hotel which would become their base of operations.

Approximately nineteen hours later Joanna Moore received the overnight package via special courier (Art has tools) from Beijing, China. The package contained vacuum-sealed bags of Freedom power bars and two plastic bottles of Freedom water. The courier had special handling instructions and been designated to notify Joanna of the status of the package. When her phone beeped the message that the package was at the Dallas terminal awaiting a RiverMoore pickup - she already had a van waiting. This van had a sealed and pressurized rear containment area, to protect the driver.

She was prepared in a quarantine suit, waiting for the arrival of the van with its possibly lethal contents to be transferred to the safety airlock entrance of the lab. She took the package directly to the decontamination area of the laboratory before opening it to reveal the contents that would need to be quickly moved to the cleanroom where these contents would be scrutinized and tested.

The area had been prepared for this arrival and the most stringent protocols were already defined in anticipation of its danger. This preparation would be a lot of wasted effort if Art happened to be wrong in his suspicion.

Unfortunately, he had not been wrong. What Joanna discovered in the testing was an unfamiliar dormant virus embedded into the rice of the Freedom Power bars. The virus seemed to be the same in the differently packaged items. The Freedom Water, however, had a different virus in it, it was virulent and active.

She immediately called Emmett Rankin. "Emmett, we need the government on something big. I just finished preliminary testing on a product called Freedom Power Bar – it is labeled as manufactured in Hong Kong, with messaging indicating it is sold to raise funds for the Hong Kong freedom fighters for democracy. The rice in this product is GMO and it contains a dormant virus – not our

HVD, but it seems to be a hybrid. You need to stop the public from buying these 'power bars'. And you need to get U.S. Customs and the Department of Commerce involved to prevent this crap from getting to our stores."

Rankin, "Holy crap, Joanna, I'm going to start making calls right now!"

Joanna, "There's something else – a liquid virus in bottles of water, but I've got to do more testing on that. The liquid seems to be a different strain of the virus – and it is being used to poison the Chinese freedom protestors. It is being represented as a product from the USA. I think they are trying to kill their protestors and possibly incite avarice toward the USA at the same time. I'm going to have to get back to you after I get more testing done. I'm growing samples now.

The primary thing you need to do is stop any USA import or consumption of the 'Freedom' packaging variety. I'm going to text you images of the packaging of the power bars that are supposed to be here or due to be here soon. I believe you will need to advise President Hominy as it relates to the blocking of the imports. I'm going to get the Savior Unit on tracking how much of this crap has reached us and where it went. Emmett, I can't emphasize enough how dangerous this material is – far more virulent than the RMV2030."

Rankin, "I'll assemble a PSA team but I'd like to ask you to please keep me informed on every testing result. I don't think this is something to be handled with phone calls to the President. I'm going to need to see POTUS in person. If the Chinese government is behind this it could be an act of War! He'll want a thorough investigation."

Joanna had her team currently growing cultures and assembling lab animals to begin testing as soon as the cultures were finished.

ART AND GOOSE
ON THE JOB

Art and Goose have a room in a hotel just a mile away from the location that Stephanie Wolff and Chuck Delphi are staying. Goose has tools and is linked to the cameras throughout the streets and buildings of Beijing, all programmed with facial recognition to spot any movement of these two targets.

It's interesting, thought Art, *Chuck hasn't left his room at the hotel and though Stephanie departed with two men and a woman, 20 hours ago, neither she nor they had returned yet.*

"Goose, will you please set up that laptop to let me review the street footage. I think we need to find out where Miss Wolff went. And perhaps you can find some information on any possible activity around Mr. Delphi's room."

Goose, "`Checking Art human`"

Art, "Goose, you can call me Art if you wish."

Goose, One blink – " `'Art if you wish'` - `Longer than 'Art human'` "

Art, "Goose, we need to work on our communications ok? Call me ART period."

Goose blinks blinks blinks " 'Art Period' longer than 'Art human' "

Slightly frustrated Art says, "Just call me ART"

Goose,

> *Webster: humor. something that is or is designed to be comical or amusing often a temporary state of mind imposed especially by circumstances*

"Goose made humor, Art." One blink.

Art chuckled, "Oh Goose – you got me – that was funny."

Goose, "Thank you, Art. Goose learns."

Art, "Yes you do Goose, do you have video from the time they went into their rooms?"

Art steps to the monitor and sees Delphi, entering the hotel room with his carry-on bag. As he fast-forwards the video, there is no activity related to that room number for nearly three hours until the appearance of a tall, very light-skinned, Chinese lady and two young girls that appear to be twins. Chuck admitted them into the room wearing a robe.

Art, "Goose, please tell me what you observe when you look at Delphi and the faces of the females also."

Goose backs the video up and frame by frame observes each movement.

Goose, "Woman identified as Miss Cha."

Art, "What?? How can you know her name? Goose"

Goose, "Biometrics identify Miss Cha."

Art, "What about the twins? Do you have biometrics on them?"

Goose, "No twins – Art."

Art, "They look like twins girls Goose."

Goose, "No Art – red is Su Lee – age 27 green is Lim Cha – age 29. Miss Cha – age 47 mother of Lim Cha – father unknown."

Art, "They look like teenagers!"

Goose, "`False image Art.`"

Moving on with the video footage – the mother Miss Cha leaves twenty minutes later. It was another thirty minutes that went by before a new character came to the door bringing a small cart with a covered basket. The man was large – and imposing looking. The door is opened by Lim Cha wearing nothing but a green band on her wrist.

Art, "Goose, does biometrics identify the employment status of these people?"

Goose, "`Yes, Art. Comfort Escort. Would Art like Goose to search Comfort Escort?`

Art, "NO Goose – that's not necessary thank you!"

As Art continued to parse through the video footage, the twins seemed to depart several times, always separately but sometimes escorted by the large man. It seems that Chuck was being comforted at all times by one or more of the three escorts. Unless Delphi jumped out of the 43rd story window, he had not left the bedroom.

Art, "Goose, please set your program to access and continuously monitor this room, then we will see what we can find about Miss Wolff."

Goose, "`Goose has tools - More Delphi footage.`"

Art, "We saw footage up to present – Mr. Delphi is still in the room."

Goose, "`Goose has tools. Footage in room.`"

Art, "WHAT the HELL??? The hotel has a video inside the bedroom?", said Art.

Goose, "`Which room Art?`"

Art, "What? What do you mean which room?"

Goose, "`Goose has tools. Footage in all rooms. Which room Art?`"

As the video turned X-rated, Art said, "Goose, perhaps you should not see this."

It didn't really matter to Goose though. Goose had not

been programmed for domestic service. Art didn't watch the entire footage, there was more than enough evidence that Delphi was loaded on drugs and sufficiently 'comforted' that he wasn't going anywhere.

Now Art turned his attention on finding Stephanie as he waited for a call from Joanna in Texas. She was going to be calling him back with the results of that material they had sent to her for testing.

He suspected Stephanie's departure was also with Comfort Escorts, but her continued absence from her room was concerning to him. He wanted very much to dispatch these two Americans and the Chinese Dr. Yīshēng, himself.

Returning to the video at the hotel, Goose moved the monitor image of the suite registered to Stephanie and parsed the video until the arrival of the woman and two men.

Goose, "`Goose is unable to get biometrics on the visitors. Pupils are dilated unable to scan, Art`"

Art, "It's ok Goose, do you have room footage?"

Goose, One blink.

Art watched the footage, as Stephanie takes a call from the bath, and shortly after there is the arrival of the three visitors. There is chatting and drinks and finger food while the female does Stephanie's hair and makeup before the four of them depart.

Art, "Goose, is there street footage that we can track where they went?"

Goose, "`Checking, yes - one stop`"

Art, "Address Goose and what can you tell me about the location – is it a business?"

Goose, "`House of Comfort and Joy - Members-only`"

Art, "Can we get footage to discover what time they entered and if they exited?"

Goose, "**Yes No**"

Art, "What? What is Yes No?"

Goose, "**Yes enter No exit**"

Just then the phone rang. "Yes, I know it is the middle of your day Joanna. What's the news on the water and power bars?"

Joanna, "Well it is bad – the water has an active virus in it – the power bars are made with genetically modified rice that contains a hybrid form of a virus that comes out of its spore form when ingested. Both are lethal. I've got DEA stopping and seizing all imports of the power bars as well as any Chinese rice imports.

There's no evidence whatsoever of the bottles of 'Freedom Water' being bottled, distributed, or exported in or from the USA. It looks like that's intended for anti-USA propaganda. Kill off the freedom fighters, blame it on the U.S. What kind of resources are you going to need to take down the facilities that are bottling and manufacturing?"

Art, "Joanna, if you will put Josh onto the task of getting me locations, I will work on putting together teams to take the facilities down. Chuck Delphi and Stephanie Wolff are here and they are in trouble. Goose has intercepted some phone conversations. Apparently, Darla Avery (CIA) and Robert Hoge are the last of the U.S. DComm Group. I think that Hominy is going to have to get the Department of Justice to lock them up. I'd love to take them out myself, but that will have to wait. There's bigger fish to fry here with the manufacturing. If DOJ can keep them locked down, I will be able to make sure they never see the light of day when I get finished over here."

Joanna, "I can talk to Rankin to get movement on Avery and Hoge, that's not in my wheelhouse. What do you mean Delphi and Wolff are 'in trouble'?"

Art, "Well apparently Doctor Yīshēng is keeping them 'entertained'. These high-class hotels keep video of everything and the entertainment is triple X rated – perhaps for purposes of extortion. I can have Goose send the material, but it is not something to be reviewed in mixed company. It's pretty perverse, Joanna."

Joanna, "Ok, Art, I get the message, have Goose send the material encrypted with the MSA recommission code. Josh and I are the only ones who know this number. I will make sure it is stored in a very secure place. Thank you for the warning. So are those two ever going to leave China?"

Art paused a moment and then replied, "Joanna, from what I know of these people, I don't think so. What's happening to them now will only get worse and they might be wishing they were dead. Send a message to my phone or Goose if you get that DOJ thing taken care of."

Joanna, "Will do Art, be safe."

CHUCK DELPHI - EARLIER
ENTERTAINMENT AND ADDICTION

It had been a long flight over to China and the time spent in meetings had been tedious. Conferencing with the States meant that they had to be present in the middle of the night (Chinese Central Time) to attend. He was pretty sure it would take some time for him to adjust to this time zone, but if he was going to need to be up all night for a meeting, it made sense for him to just learn to become a night owl.

His hotel room was a luxury suite with every possible amenity, including bottles of his favorite scotch beside the basket of fruits and candy dishes. Of course, the room was equipped with the most sophisticated videography equipment to observe his every move and conversation while he was there, but he didn't know that. He was of the misimpression that he was on the same side as the Chinese.

After a relaxing shower, he stretched out on the bed for a little nap while he waited to see what kind of taste Dr. Yīshēng had in women. He quickly slipped into a peaceful sleep that was interrupted two hours later by a soft knock on the door. He grabbed a robe and answered the door to find a matched pair of the sweetest looking little china dolls standing in front of a young woman.

The lady introduced herself as Miss Lin Cha. She explained to him, in very good English, that if he approved, these twin girls would be his escorts for the evening or as long as he chose to spend with them. She continued that if they were not acceptable to his taste, she would ask for a description of what would be more suitable to him.

The girls were perfect, like little twin dolls – wearing the same clothing other than the fact that one had a red band on her wrist, while the other wore a green band. He told Miss Cha, that these girls were perfect except he wasn't dressed to go out, so they would need to wait.

Miss Cha, "Mr. Dick Delphi, you do not need to worry yourself with your clothing. These girls are trained to attend all your needs. If you are not too tired to dine out, they will escort you to a location to provide your choice of cuisine, or if you choose to order room service, this hotel has very good food service to be delivered to the comfort of your lovely suite."

She introduced each girl to him at this time, pointing to the one with the red band on her wrist saying as a means of introduction, "This sweet thing is named Sokk Yu – this is pronounced like Sock – such as you wear on your foot. You see she wears the red band on her wrist."

Then she pointed to the other and continued, "And this is Fokk Yu, you see she wears the green band. Do not be concerned if you get them confused and call out the wrong name, I, make the mistake if I do not look at the band on their wrists. I'm told that sometimes they like to play a game and switch their bands when they are entertaining." Miss Cha then laughed a small melodic laugh at her own innuendo-laden joke.

The girls looked so young, he felt that he must inquire if Miss Cha would be staying as a chaperone. Miss Cha only laughed and said these girls were trained to attend to his comfort needs unless he desired her presence also.

Well, thinks Chuck, *I didn't want to be greedy*, so he decided to dismiss Miss Cha thinking, *Perhaps another time.*

Miss Cha left so that Mr. Dick Delphi might begin days of entertainment with the twin dolls names Sokk Yu and Fokk Yu. He didn't know they were not really twins, nor what their real names were.

The 'dollies' as Chuck had decided to refer to them, Red Dollie and Green Dollie', were indeed eager to attend to his comfort.

Chuck, "So my little dollies, have you had your dinner? I can order food to be brought to the room unless you would prefer to go out for the night."

The dollies answered as one, "Our pleasure is to bring joy to you Mr. Dickie… What will please Mr. Dickie?"

Chuck, "You prefer to call me Dickie? My name is Chuck but if you want to call me Dickie, you could call me Daddy Dickie."

Red Dollie named Sokk smiled a secret smile and said, "Mr. Daddy Dickie, Sokk would love to please you. Perhaps Mr. Daddy Dickie will come to the other room while Fokk orders food for all of us. If this will please Mr. Daddy Dickie?"

That would please him very much, and off he went with Sokk Yu – red Dollie to the bedroom where she provided comfort in a manner most similar to her name. While that was happening, a very virile young man called Dog, arrived with a basket of food and other toys of pleasure for the events to be coming later in the evening. By the time the food arrived, Daddy Dickie was soundly sleeping after the professional ministrations of Sokk Yu – red Dollie.

So Fokk and Dog ate and prepared the next phase of the comfort to be provided to Chuck. The basket included a variety of opiates suitable to be smoked, injected, ingested, or infused via a nether orifice. Chuck was sleeping so soundly, that he didn't notice when Sokk left him to eat then return with the other two, to prepare him for a sexual onslaught beyond his wildest imagination. He only woke briefly to realize that he was being sodomized by something in a mask that looked like a dog and raped by both of the dollies at the same time. Each time he woke from the drugs, they were there – in different positions of attention. The comfort team was well paid to insure that Mr. Daddy Dickie was totally addicted to the things they brought to abuse him.

When Darla Avery or Robert Hoge called from America, their phone calls went to the front desk who assured the caller that Mr. Delphi would receive the message when he returned to his suite. Of course, all of the fantasy escapades were captured in high definition digital quality from multiple positions throughout the rooms to ensure the most complete and detailed recordings of the abuse.

Chuck had no idea what was happening to him. By the time Art had intercepted the video recordings, Chuck had been subjected to twenty hours of this insanity.

STEPHANIE WOLFF - EARLIER
ENTERTAINMENT AND ADDICTION

Stephanie wished she had been able to bring Dave Tillis and Beau Clark along with her. Dave Tillis had been her NSA white hat, black hat, go-to guy – a computer genius. Beau (her Ragin Cajun) was intended to be her boy-toy for a while. But that damn Savior Unit interrupted the DComm Group Project Clearcut and sadly, her plans for Beau were never realized. Perhaps, she thinks Dr. Yīshēng will find some suitable Asian replacement to fulfill her fantasies.

She went to her suite to freshen up and was pleasantly surprised to see a lovely tray of fresh fruit and a bottle of sparkling wine chilling in an ice bucket along with an assortment of other beverages from which she could choose.

As she was soaking in the walk-in tub of steaming mineral water, the suite phone rang on the wall next to her.

She answered quickly, "Yes, may I help you?"

Caller, "Miss Stephanie? My name is Lien. I have with me Jian and Shunguan to escort you if it pleases you to be entertained. Doctor Yīshēng told me that you may wish to choose to dine or go shopping and we are here to escort you if you so wish. We are in the lobby area if this is a convenient time for you, Miss Stephanie."

Stephanie, "Oh I am soaking in the tub, but you are welcome to come up. I have not had dinner, but there is food here in the suite."

Lien, "We will be up directly Miss Stephanie, thank you." And the line was disconnected. They knew she was soaking in the tub before they made the call.

Stephanie quickly toweled herself off and put on a simple shift with no underwear. When the three arrived, Stephanie was pleasantly surprised at the trio. Lien did the introductions. "This is Jian, he is a very good protector.' She then points to the diminutive one who seemed very shy and said, 'This is Shunguan, he speaks English not as well, I think not because he does not know the language but because he loses his voice in the presence of such a beautiful woman", and she laughed, "My name is Lien." Lien was stunning, with the creamiest ivory colored skin and eyes the shape of perfect almonds but the color of shining onyx.

Stephanie showed the three to the dining area and suggested that they were welcome to eat or drink while she dried her hair. The large one named Jian poured a drink for the very shy Shunguan and Lien said, "Miss Stephanie, I would be pleased to dry your hair, then if you wish to see the city of Beijing I know of a very special place you might enjoy unless you are too tired after your long journey."

Stephanie very much enjoyed having her hair and makeup done by Lien. During this preparation to go out, Stephanie asked if the names had meanings or translations in English.

Lien, "Oh, yes. Jian, the protector that is here with us, his name means Strong and Indefatigable. Shunguan means Obedient. My name means Lotus. Perhaps so named for the color of my skin."

Stephanie, "That is LOVELY, I would love it if you

would give me a Chinese name that is easier to say than Miss Stephanie!"

Lien, "I would call you Huan – this means Joy or Satisfaction. Does this name please you, Miss Stephanie?"

Stephanie, now called Huan, "Thank you, that will be my name for this night then!" She had no idea how long this night would be.

It was after 10 PM in China when they left the hotel, but Huan didn't mind, she was invigorated and excited at the prospect of exploring a country from a pleasure perspective rather than a business one. Their first stop was an enormous building – with a relatively small dining area on the first floor. The tables were set in what might be considered buffet style in the USA, but different as there were no rows of chafing dishes lined side by side. The lights were dim and Lien made suggestions of items to try. It seemed that each item was meant to be eaten as an appetizer. She tried a variety of fishy tasting items – some of which she recognized as squid, octopus, calamari, and shrimp. Each sample was taken in small single bites, so she might enjoy more variety.

The next table was set with plates of what seemed to be a variety of insects including something resembling a centipede which she passed by. Lien pointed, with hand-carved chopsticks, at a plate of the cooked scorpion. "Please Huan, this is a delicacy that you must not pass by. First, you must bite the head off this treat, then as you hold the body, you will bite with your teeth the stinger, it is safe Huan, I will demonstrate." And she did demonstrate exactly as she had said.

So Huan followed the instruction. The head of the scorpion tasted slightly like anise or licorice with a delightful crunch of the outer shell. She then bit off the stinger in another single crunch. The flavor was different, the stinger flavor tasted to her much like clove, pungent, and savory. She felt an almost instant flush in her head that was foreign to her but not altogether unpleasant. She thought to herself, *well that wasn't so bad* but she wasn't aware that she spoke these words out loud. Lien leaned to her ear and whispered, "Not bad at all."

Huan had another sense of that flushing feeling – slightly confused whether she had thought or spoken the words and questioned whether Lien had answered the unspoken words or if she had imagined the whisper.

Throughout this dining adventure, Jian, the bulky strong one had stayed in front of the ladies and Shunguan (Obedient) had stayed a quiet respectable distance behind. But now, he stepped forward to offer from another table a small plate containing what looked like miniature kiwis. They were small orbs covered with a fuzzy outer layer. Shunguan had his head bowed in submission as he offered this treat to Miss Huan. She looked to Lien who nodded in approval and gently picked one off the plate and popped it gently into her own mouth to demonstrate the correct way to eat.

When she turned to take one for herself, Shunguan was holding one in the chopsticks, his eyes downward, waiting for her to take the orb from his offering.

Huan, "Thank you Shunguan, you are very kind, is this a favorite of yours?"

Shunguan, "If it is your pleasure for it to be my favorite, it will so be Miss Huan." And he gently moved the orb toward her mouth which she slowly opened to receive the offering. Oh the inside - when she bit down - burst a gooey fluid that did taste like some fruit. "Thank you Shunguan, I would be pleased if you were to feed me another."

She continued thus, asking him to feed her until she realized that Lien and Jian were no longer present. She had a moment of confusion, then she asked where the others had gone.

Shunguan, "They went to prepare for the costume event Miss Huan, I am to take you there when you are done dining."

As she looked around she saw that the room was filled with people wearing costumes as they dined. She was pretty sure she was now high on something she'd eaten because she was easily confused.

Huan, "But you see I have no costume!"

Shunguan, "There is a place for you to choose one Miss Huan, we will go there now if you are ready."

And he gently took her arm to guide her because she was intoxicated with many types of insect venom now – the fuzzy kiwi looking orbs she had so loved were the bodies of tarantula spiders.

HUAN
THE COSTUME SHOP

Shunguan guided Huan to the elevator and up they went several floors. Huan had no idea how many, but she was held gently though firmly by her guide Shunguan. He led her to a room that had walls covered with masks. She looked at many and held them up to her face while Shunguan held a mirror for her in the softly lit room.

Huan, "Shunguan, tell me the truth – what mask is the most beautiful for this Stephanie Huan! You know my other name is Wolff, do you think I need a mask that looks like a vicious animal?"

Shunguan – shyly looking at the floor, "Miss Huan, is much too beautiful for the face of a dog. The Chinese name you have chosen is one of satisfaction and joy. This humble Shunguan thinks Miss Haun needs more."

So Huan tried on mask after mask – some with feathers, others with sequins and glittering patterns. As she modeled each mask – she tried to look into Shunguan's eyes to find approval, but he only looked sadder with each new mask.

Huan, "I am not satisfied, or with joy, Shunguan, I think I want to eat more of those fuzzy balls that made me smile!

Can you get them for me Shunguan?"

He just looked down and stepped toward the door where he had set a plate of them earlier, unnoticed by her in her quest for the perfect mask. She patiently waited for him to slowly feed her two of the orbs, then she cried out, "Shunguan, I must find a costume for the party, you said I would be going to a party!"

Shunguan, "Please Miss Huan, take my arm and I will take you to a place to find the perfect costume of joy and satisfaction that will honor Miss Huan."

He escorted her then to another room with an entrance from this mask room. Much to her surprise, Lien was waiting for her. Lien spoke in Chinese to Shunguan who bowed and stepped quickly out of this room. Lien was wearing leather which was the color of her skin, giving her the illusion of being naked. As Huan looked around the room she saw it was filled with all manner of leather articles – not just masks.

Lien, "Shunguan has treated you properly? If he has not, we will flog him, he is sometimes weak like a flower."

Huan, "Oh I was annoyed because he could not help me find the proper mask for the costume party."

Lien, "Well then Miss Haun, you will need some proper costume for both your joy and satisfaction."

With Lien's guidance, Huan was clothed in black leather. The pants were extremely tight – with the buttocks area missing. The straps from the front to the rear had buckles to cinch up and ensure the most pleasingly plump buttocks proud and immobile. They also seemed designed to expose the pubic area which, fortunately, Huan always kept free of hair. The vest was only a vest in front with openings for the breasts to protrude – also tightened with the buckles to ensure extreme pressure on the exposed nipples. As Lien repeatedly tightened the straps, she continuously fondled the exposed flesh, pushing and pulling to ensure the perfect roundness and hardness of the various areas. The final part of the costume was a leather mask that covered the top of the head and face – leaving the eyes and mouth exposed, but the chin was covered. The mask had gold rings on the chin and the top. As Lien had been making adjustments she had also been applying oil to the skin of the exposed areas – oil that contained sexual enhancement chemicals that were highly addictive.

When Lien led Huan from the room, they went to another where Shunguan and Jian were waiting for them. There was no costume party. Shunguan was no longer shy and afraid. The rings of the mask were used to control her head and mouth, be it open or closed depending on the manner of rape at the moment. She was raped repeatedly by all three of the comfort escorts and she loved every minute as the drugs and abuse continued beyond her consciousness.

Huan (no longer referred to by the name Stephanie Wolff) had been escorted to a private club in Beijing which was frequented by a very elite class of citizens. There they exercised the most private level of discretion enjoying the baser and taboo sexual behaviors in privacy. She became a willing participant in the engagement of these drug-induced behaviors. She used, and was used, in fantasies by many.

Weeks from now, when Huan is no longer interesting in the sophisticated clientele of the private club in Beijing, she will be transported to Thailand where she will be sold into the sex slave market and continue to be drugged and more severely abused - until she is no more.

Art knew where she was and could have easily removed or quickly dispatched her to prevent the continuation of the abuse, but he chose to let it continue. He would have people in Thailand follow her path, but he would not allow her to return to the United States under any circumstances.

CHAIRMAN ZHÁNG WEI JUN

Good news came to the attention of the Chairman that the camps were, one by one, becoming empty. The rioting youth of the country, marching for democracy, could soon be apprehended and moved to refill the camps. They refused to go for inoculations and they wore their masks as they marched and waved their flags demanding freedom. It was time for the Chairman to have them rounded up and put into the camps where they could eat and die or simply starve to death, but the end must be the same – they must die. He knew from past experience that simple incarceration was not sufficient to break the spirit and determination of the foolish ones.

The Chairman had approved the construction of multiple facilities for the research, development, and manufacture of a variety of new agents. The strategies to spread the new strain of the virus were:

> 1.) Manufacturing of 'tear gas' bombs, no longer containing tear gas but now containing the HVD virus that will become the floating fog which will be impossible to avoid breathing. The virus infused

smoke will be inhaled and will leave residue on surfaces of apparel, including clothing, hats, masks, and shoes. All these items carried the new Chinese synthetic version of HVD to the homes of the rioting youth to further infect friends and family members.

2.) All law enforcement, military, and their family members will receive their anti-virus vaccines prior to smoke bomb deployment. They will no longer need gas masks to protect them as they had when dispensing tear gas bombs but the public should not notice the change in the enforcement gear.

3.) The dissenters would be receiving truckloads of water bottles and individually packaged chocolate coated rice power bars. These shipments were labeled FREEDOM with a small USA flag on the labels. The people will believe that the trucks of FREEDOM gifts came from America in support of their quest for democracy.

4.) The guests at political and ethnic re-education camps will be served food and beverages containing the hybrid strain of the HVD.

5.) The packaging process will also prepare for export to the USA, power bars, named Freedom, bearing labels with the image of the Hong Kong flag. These power bars will include, in English, a well-written message thanking the American's for their purchase, with a statement that the proceeds of the purchase went to support the Hong Kong freedom fighters.

6.) The Chairman has the Ministry of Trade

personnel negotiating a very attractive price for the GMO rice exports to the USA. The Americans will buy these items at grocery and Just-a-Dollar stores. The crunchy rice bars are being made with small quantities of the GMO rice developed and grown in China. The purchasers would be proud to spend a dollar to help those struggling 'over there' fighting for their freedom from communism. The bags of contaminated rice would further ensure the destruction of the enemy.

The DComm Group cowards who had fled to China were nearly useless to the Chairman. Their addictions and abuses were sufficient that they had but one value to the Chinese government. If the USA demanded their return, they would receive videos to realize that further demand on the Chairman would be met with the world-wide public display of the depravity of the vial Laowai – an embarrassment to the 'precious' United States of America on the world stage.

The Chairman did not need to see the videos to know what entertainment was provided to Miss Stephanie Wolff and Mr. Delphi. These two were just simple examples of how weak the Americans were - proof of why China would soon be in control of the world. China had waited and planned for generations to take the world for itself, the time was finally in sight.

ART, GOOSE AND DA
ADDING A NEW TEAM MEMBER

Art realizes that he no longer needs to be concerned about monitoring Chuck Delphi and Stephanie Wolff. Now, he and Goose turn their attention to preparing the plan to put an end to the viral destruction about to be executed from China on both Chinese nationals and other countries including the United States of America.

Dr. Yīshēng had in service, a Chinese version of MSA – Goose. Goose was able to establish communications with the MSA070771LMC.

Goose, `"Art, Goose has established communications link with MSA070771LMC – Chinese medical services assistant to Doctor Yīshēng – Beijing.`

`Does Art have questions for MSA-LMC?"`

Art, "Goose that is great news – does LMC have information about the HVD?"

Goose, `"Goose requires interface with MSA-LMC for purpose of data sharing – language confirmation."`

Art, "Is the MSA allowed to leave its work location? Do

we need to find a way into the laboratory for you to make this happen?"

Goose continued, "No – Yes – Art must work on communication – humor Art."

Art, "Goose, are you considering a career in comedy? So where is the laboratory where the virus is made?"

Goose,

Webster: comedy: humorous entertainment

"Comedy, Art? Goose must research comedy. Laboratory where virus is made – Dongguan 1886 miles from Beijing."

Damn, thinks Art, *I guess we're going to have to lay out our travel plans.*

He calls a local operative named Da. Da is ex-Chinese military and a technician with many skills including disguise expertise and connections to an extensive network of skilled individuals. Art is going to need to blend in with the locals if he is going to have a chance of entering the Dongguan Lab.

Art, "Da, Damone here – in Beijing, I've got a mission up in Dongguan that I'm going to need some help with. There is a laboratory up there that I need to penetrate and link some communications inside. Then I have a much bigger set of projects that will need a lot of coordination. Can you meet us in Dongguan?"

Da, "Yes, of course Art. Anything you need Da can help."

Art, "Great, I have a droid with me. I'll need a robot repair uniform for the nearest reputable firm to that area, and I'm gonna need to resemble a local to get in there with my droid. So get me a uniform, some credentials, and whatever makeup tricks you have."

Da, "You are lucky Da is so skilled." Da gave him the name of a hotel nearest to the Dongguan Labs and said he'd book it under his name and send Art the room number as soon as it was ready. Art agreed to meet Da the following day at noon and hung up quickly to make the air reservations for their trip to Dongguan.

This wouldn't be the first time that Art had disguised his face to look Asian. Da was waiting at the hotel with a case of makeup and a uniform complete with badges to turn Art into what appeared to be a Chinese local robotics repair service agent.

ART AND DA
THE MISSIONS

Back at the 'hotel' Da had debugged and disabled the cameras in the room before Art and Goose first arrived. This exercise was repeated when they returned from Dongguan - before they began their strategy planning. Art explained that this laboratory is where the synthetic HVD is manufactured in one of the buildings on the campus. The material is processed for three needs.

Some of the material is shipped to a bottling and packaging plant located at Tianjin which is 114 kilometers from Beijing. The bottling process injects lethal doses of the virus into plain water. Then the infected bottles of water are sealed and labeled Freedom water. The bottles of water are being dispensed for free to the freedom marchers in Beijing.

Another smaller building on the Lab campus is where the material is packaged into the small smoke bomb canisters. These would be distributed to the police and military for use in dealing with the freedom marchers.

The third building is where the synthetic HVD is packaged into vaccine vials for injections to be shipped for use at the re-education camps and elsewhere.

Art continued with his briefing of the missions. "So then we have the issue of the Freedom Bars. Da, these are made and packaged in Shanghai. They look like a 'power bar' made from crunchy rice and chocolate, but the rice is GMO rice – grown here in China with a dormant virus that will go live when ingested. From what I've discovered, this Shanghai plant packages 'Freedom Bars' to distribute for free to the Chinese freedom marchers and labeled to look like they are gifted by the U.S. They are also packaged for export to the U.S., transversely represented as 'Thank You' bars and as fundraiser promotional items to support the Chinese freedom marchers. And, somewhere there is a place where the rice is being grown or treated to add the virus. I have some U.S. friends trying to narrow down a possible location."

Da, "Art, it looks like we need several teams to take this stuff down. You not going to be able to stay under radar hopping around airports like that. Somebody will notice."

"I know," said Art, "I already have Jake, Jimbo, Wham, and Lightnin' on their way to Beijing. Wham and Lightnin' won't be so noticeable, but Jake and Jimbo are whiter than me. The four of them are munitions technicians and we will need to keep them pretty much under the radar as well. I'm going to need two munitions experts down near Beijing for the Tianjin operation and at least one for the Shanghai takedown, and I figured one up at Dongguan. You think that if I pair Jake and Jimbo with some Asians, they wouldn't look so out of place?"

Da, "Well I brought list of Chinese operatives to consider." He pulled a list from his jacket pocket.

"Dai and Feng – they are Shi warriors, with martial arts and swords being specialties, good for quiet close work.

Jiaguo and Gan are my weapons guys.

Longwei and Duyi are best drivers if we need to get in and out of facilities. They are great with trucks too. They can thread needle with loaded semi and put those things exactly where well-loaded truck can do most damage.

Deshi, Hungqu, and Dingbang are fearless ones; I think you want them on Dongguan Lab takedown."

Art, "We are going to need recon at the sites before we finalize the logistics. I'll need you to set up a meet with the team."

Da, "You betcha Art. I set up a hotel location for recon meeting, won't be nice like this – but we not risk debugging room every time someone step out for a smoke." With that plan in place, Da leaves to make the Beijing arrangements and pull the team of operatives together for a first meeting.

BLACK OPS MEETING

The group met as a team for the first time at the Beijing "hotel". The location was in the shady district of Beijing to protect their anonymity that would have been challenging in the luxurious suites of the big tourist locations. The rooms had been quickly checked for surveillance devices. Some were found that may have served purposes decades ago but were no longer functional. Hotel services could be requested at the front desk if there happened to be someone not otherwise engaged. Goose had tools to provide round the clock security and this place was well suited for privacy or prostitution but not cleanliness or comfort. As each team arrived, Da handed them a disposable phone.

In attendance:

Art Damone (USA – black ops)
Jake and Jimbo (UK and USA – munitions specialists)
Wham and Ligntnin (Asian-American – munitions)
Da (China – disguise and technology)
Dai and Feng (China – Shi warriors)

Jiaguo and Gan (China - weapons specialists)
Longwei and Duyi (stunt and truck drivers)
Deshi, Hungqu, and Dingbang (multi-faceted ops)

Art, "Before we talk about the installations we need to recon and takedown, I need to ask if anyone here can fly a plane, like a crop duster style? The reason I ask this is that I do not doubt that we can take out our building targets – but we have a possible location of a rice farm growing GMO rice. We need to ensure that they don't grow more of the lethal GMO rice, so we may need to sterilize the rice fields. Goose can provide satellite photos and GPS coordinates of the approximate location, but we need a way to spray the land to prevent accidental growth of any rice seed that may have gotten scattered during the harvesting process."

Da quickly stated that he had contacts that could see to this immediately and promptly texted someone.

Art, "Good, moving on then I think it is best to outline our targets and define our teams. Goose has assisted me on this list."

Goose went to the window and closed the blackout window coverings, or what was left of them, turned and said, `"To prevent spying` Art"

Webster: Spy: to watch secretly usually for hostile purposes

Art had to suppress a laugh as he explained to the team, "Goose is learning to be a Black Ops support operative. Thank you, Goose, for your sagacious attention to our well-being."

He looked at his watch and said to the team, "Any wagers on how long it will take?" A minute passed while the team was stifling their laughs.

Goose,

Webster: Sagacious: keen and farsighted penetration of

judgment

"Art suggesting Goose is farsighted?"

Art now had to laugh out loud. "No Goose, humor. We must return to our meeting now please." Goose recalled the Webster definition of humor.

Just as Art was about to stop this line of dialog with Goose and return to the meeting there was a knock at the door. He had previously hung the very grimy and well-worn 'do not disturb sign' on it but he went to the door. Outside the door was Soo Lin, she was four foot and nine inches tall and 90 pounds. She was wearing a short spikey pink wig and fishnet stockings below the too tight, too short skirt. Her lack of undergarments was easily recognizable through the sparkled yet threadbare spandex camisole style top.

Art opened the door. "No bed turn down, sweetie, no room service here, thank you."

The tiny Soo Lin walked right past Art into the room and saw the group of men seated there. "Ohhhh you gotta lotta big men here, Soo Lin need mo money to do big men. You biggie men lika train with little girl?"

Art didn't notice that Da was suppressing a laugh. Art said, "Oh no miss Soo, there has been a mistake, I did not request comfort service, perhaps you have come to the wrong room."

Soo Lin now appeared to become very angry. "I come all way to this room, now somebody gonna pay, mister USA bigshot!"

Da is now laughing so hard that tears are running down his cheeks. Goose looks back and forth at the exchange that includes confusion by Art, false anger by the female, and uncontained laughter by Da.

Da, "Stop, Stop Soo! Art, this is my cousin Soo Lin, she is a pilot. She is here to get coordinates for the rice fields you need to be sterilized." He is now wiping the tears off his cheeks and composing himself.

Goose looked at Art, "Hah, humor, hah Art. Goose understands joke now. Art, Soo Lin pretends to be comfort escort girl to trick Art. Art is confused."

Art, "STOP Goose, you do not need to explain to me!" The entire team including Soo Lin was now laughing at the very embarrassed Art.

"I'd like to return to our meeting if you have all had your daily dose of entertainment. Welcome Soo, you will hold a special place in my mission log when this is done."

Art continued, "Soo do you have access to material to sterilize the soil of these fields? We can't leave them to accidentally grow new GMO rice that may have been left behind during the harvesting process."

Goose interrupted, "Various forms available: 'Sterizal' (phenol), Brays Emulsion and Armillatox (cresylic acid), also Jeyes fluid (tar oil plus vegetable oil). Does Miss Soo human have access? Goose can research distributor for these."

Soo, responding to both Art and Goose, "Da and I can manage, I need know GPS coordinates and what night you want it done. Best time for spraying is at nighttime because chemicals sink to earth faster than in heat of day."

Art, "Soo, we have some idea of where the rice field is but have to confirm with reconnaissance of the area. That will be happening after this meeting."

She asked, "Then I wait for location. Is there anything else you need me to do? I have other talents." She looks at Art and makes a lewd grinding gesture with her hips before breaking into a hysterical laugh because she again made him blush as with his earlier mistake. She knew that she would be spending more time with him when these ops were done.

Soo had served in the Chinese Aviation division; she had joined the military very young by falsifying her identity and age. She learned the mechanical detail of every plane ever flown from any Asian continent. Christ, she could build an airplane if she wanted to, But since her family had been arrested for accused crimes against the state, her personal mission was revenge and the only way to effect that was to learn. Knowledge was power and she was a very powerful little woman. Her family was most surely long dead in the camps, but her memory was very much alive.

Well, there is the dispatch of Chuck Delphi, and Stephanie Wolff thinks Art. But he doesn't say this out loud – he would prefer to finish off those two, himself. They were instrumental in the attempt to Clearcut the USA and it would please him very much to decommission them.

To Soo, he says, "There is a private jet sitting in a hangar at Beijing airport. This plane will need a specialty program loaded into the navigational system and the transponder rigged to be disabled at a strategic point in time. We're going to handle this later in the week. Is this something you can help with?"

Soo, "I can do these things. You need a plane to disappear. Goose, put location and plane identification number in separate file with date and time. I assume flight plan will be different than one provided to tower. So there will be two flight plans – please identify one as Tower plan and other as Actual."

Goose, "Yes Miss Soo Lin, Goose has also added list of chemical providers with locations and hours of operation."

Now that she has her mission and documentation, she departs the room to go prepare for her tasks and wait for the go-ahead from Art. As she prepares to leave she tells Goose in Mandarin, "Soo is hot for Art" and she winks at Goose before she wags her behind as she exits the room. If Goose could smile he would have. He returns her one blink for yes. Goose then displays, on the wall, the list of targets, and possible strategies.

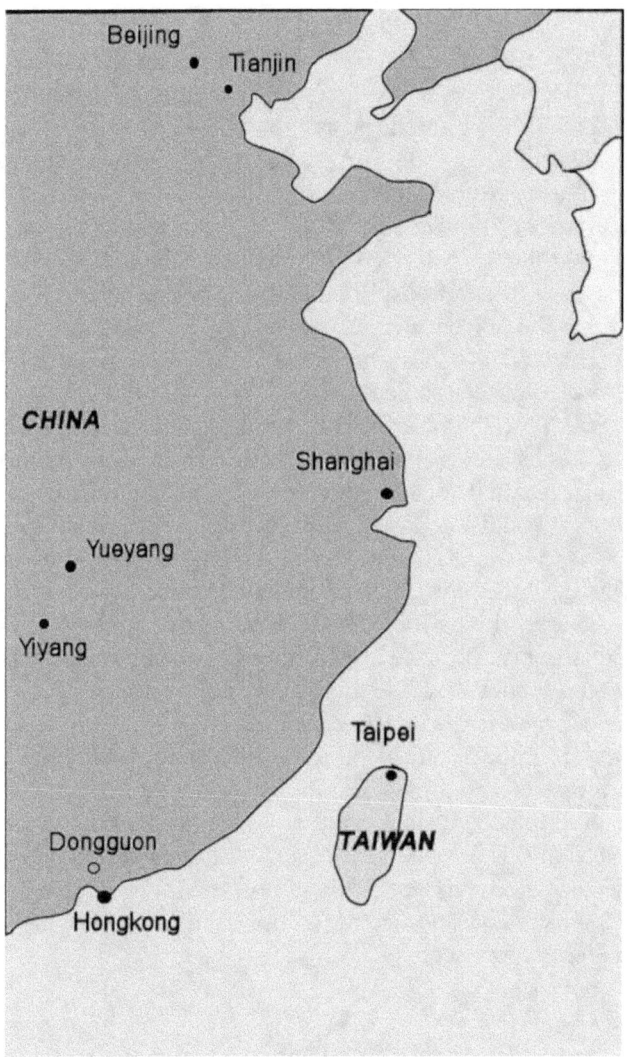

Using a laser pointer to highlight a specific topic of conversation, Art begins.

Dongguan

"We have target number one: Dongguan – laboratory. The first building at this facility manufactures the synthetic HVD which is created for multiple uses, first and foremost to kill targeted groups of the organized insurrection that desire to overthrow the communist regime in China. HVD is short for Human Viral Decommissioning and the name we are using to describe the different versions of the stuff. The virus is then transported by truck to Tianjin where it is infused in bottled water.

Then there is a second building that assembles HVD aerosol canisters similar to tear gas – to be used by the police of Beijing where the freedom fighters march. These gas bombs are simple devices with a manual pushbutton that mixes the HVD with a reagent creating an aerosol 'fog' of sorts, similar to tear gas or pepper spray, its intended goal is to be inhaled and coat the clothing of the protestors which will then infect their families when they return home. Of course, the police will be vaccinated against the HVD and have no true knowledge of the virus being dispensed in the fog bombs. Because there is no violent reaction such as pepper or tear gas, the freedom marchers will assume that these fog bombs are no threat, and continue carrying the virus to others.

And, finally, there is another building where the virus is placed into vials to be sent to any location where injections are to be administered. Right now we believe these are going to re-education camps. Goose and I are on point for the recon of the Lab."

Tianjin

"The Tianjin bottling facility is 114 kilometers from Beijing. This location bottles water mixed with the HVD from Dongguan and is bottling and labeling it as Freedom water. I'm going to need two of our munitions guys to travel there and set up shop for three days. The goal is to record all we can on the facility, traffic in and out, their security, and the surrounding area."

Wham spoke up first, "I can do this."

Then Lightnin' added, "Where Wham goes I go."

Art, "Great, I got my first two volunteers."

Shanghai

"The Shanghai target campus is located 1200 kilometers from Beijing. Our reason for this target is the manufacturing of the Freedom Bars – Chocolate covered gooey rice bars that resemble power bars. There are three buildings on the site and we need eyes on all of them and to find out which one, or if all of them, are making the bars. We know that one or more package the bars for distribution to the Chinese freedom fighters and export to the USA. We're not sure if all the buildings are involved or only one or two.

Same as the bottling plant in Tianjin, I need two more volunteers to take on this recon and gather details on all the operations, security, and area around the place that we can. The more we know the better our chance of handling all possible contingencies and getting to success.

"Jiaguo and I can take this one," said Gan. Jiaguo shook his head in the affirmative.

Art, "Then we are good on this part as well."

Rice farm

"For the rice farm, I'll be looking for someone to hang out with the locals and gather information to confirm the suspected location and then scope out the facility. We need to get this one right so we stop the production and ensure the whole farm is rendered unusable. This place is in Hunan and near the city of Yiyang, volunteers?"

Da, "I can do this. Who else will be with me?"

Deshi and Dingbang both spoke at the same time with

identical responses of, "I will."

Beijing

"There is an operation in Beijing involving the evil Dr. Yīshēng – developer of the Chinese variant of HVD. Goose, Da, and I have a plan to dispatch the doctor and his MSA with the data. But, ensuring that there is no remaining access to the formula is critical. I may need Dai or Feng, our Shi warriors, to help with some work on this project, but that will be later in the week and will involve Soo as well."

Dai jumped in first, "I got this one. Anything you need Art, Dai can do."

Art, "Dai, I'll keep you posted with what goes down and when we need you."

Art then finished with, "Some of you just need to hang back while we get the recon done and then meet back here in three days. We'll call on you as needed and Da will be the main contact. I regret that these missions are physically so distant, but all who are here are battle-tested and work great, both independently and as teams. Oh, and Jake and Jimbo, you white guys need to be especially careful to not get noticed by the authorities. Have a good time and look like tourists, but stay out of trouble for a few days."

ART AND GOOSE
THE STAKEOUT

Art and Goose took on the reconnaissance of the Dongguan Lab and the surrounding area. Using Da's connections and his ability to get just about anything they could need – Art and Goose were set up with a vantage point in an empty apartment building located on a small hill about 1/4 kilometer from the lab. They had a spotting scope, night vision goggles, a drone, food and water. While on the stakeout, Art's hotel room sat empty other than some clothing which would afford no interest to any level of curiosity. He had left a stack of comfort escort provider leaflets on the desk, so anyone entering would assume that he was otherwise occupied.

On day one they flew a sacrificial drone above the Lab on a pre-programmed path. They had the drone's camera broadcast its encrypted output to a remote repeater from which Goose could intercept the signal and record the video. The drone's travel began from well north of the Lab area and went about 1.5 kilometers to its south and 1/4 kilometer off to the east. It then circled back on the west side of the lab, so as not to be directly overhead, and onto the pre-programmed landing position in a sewage pond where the drone met its final decommissioning.

After the drone flight was completed, Art assigned Goose to surveillance of the Lab from their stationary vantage point. While Goose was monitoring the lab, Art reviewed the video from the drone and sketched out a rough layout and some notes on a tablet while sipping on a strong cup of coffee he grabbed on the way to the hideout. It would be the last hot item he'd enjoy until they returned to the hotel. He would spend more time reviewing that video and Goose's observations over the next two days.

Art, "So, Goose, how do you like your first stakeout?" Art was trying to make conversation while Goose was busy with the task of monitoring the hacked video feed from the State-run surveillance cameras surrounding the Lab area.

Goose,

> *Webster: Stakeout: surveillance maintained by the police of an area or a person suspected of criminal activity*
>
> *Webster: Like: to electronically register one's approval of something for others to see as in 'Brittany gave the post one like.'*

"Goose gives stakeout one like."

Art, "I'm glad to hear it. We're going to be here for a couple of days and nights."

Goose, "Must save humanity. Why stakeout for such long time?"

Art, "Well, we need to see what a typical day looks like around the lab, to help plan for its takedown. A couple of days and nights should be enough to know what goes on there - who comes, and when, and who leaves, and when. We'll need to blend into the normal lab routine so we can sneak in and out as needed if we have to and we need to be careful. Being careful takes time."

Goose,

Webster: Sneak: to go stealthily or furtively: SLINK

`"Is 'sneak' component of subterfuge?"`
Art, "Yup, it is,"
Goose, `"Goose gives 'sneak' one like."`
Art, "Art gives Goose one like."
If Goose could smile he would have - so he blinks once - affirmative.

Maybe it was poor planning on the part of the Chinese or just plain luck for the team, but the lab was located in an open area about 1/2 kilometer from a petrol storage tank farm and railroad load/offload station. It was also slightly downhill from the tank farm providing an almost too simple means of eliminating the target. The virus destruction is best performed via incineration and with a massive supply of flammable fuel such a short distance away, it's just about perfect. *Too perfect,* thinks Art. Of course, something would need to be done about the video surveillance in the area and there would have to be a means to ignite the fuel after figuring out how to get it to flood the area, but those were details the munitions and weapons guys would have no trouble with.

Art and Goose spent three days and two nights monitoring the lab facility and surrounding area. On the last day, Art reviewed more of the video captured by Goose and looked over his notes for some ideas to offer the team. The lab had two delivery vans that came and went several times throughout the day and they always ended up parked in a few reserved spaces near the main entrance. He gave Da a call to have one of the guys tail the vans and document their travels. The area around the lab was surrounded by a tall fence topped with razor wire, but the main entrance had a high berm that stretched partway around the facility and had one main gate. A back gate was secured but led to a grove of trees and brush, so there was no in and out at that gate. All employees came and went through the main entrance starting at 7 AM. Art counted a total of 26 individuals with three security guards. One guard always remained on the premises at night, but all lab employees were out by 8 PM.

At the top end of the Lab property, just beyond the grove of trees, some street repair work was taking place and looked to be wrapping up with fill dirt having been placed and compacted. There were several temporary concrete barricades on the road that might come in handy. Art had Goose check with the NSA guys to see if they could find out more, but a call to Da was all he needed to learn that the construction would continue through the month.

The one big concern was the plethora of surveillance in the area. It was an industrial part of Dongguan and there were lots of other types of manufacturing in the area in addition to the fuel tank farm. Once per hour at 15 minutes before the top of the hour, a security patrol vehicle would make rounds. They were in and out of the immediate area within three or four minutes, but it meant fitting the execution in a window. The State security office was located some distance away from the area which also meant they would have some amount of time before a patrol might be called in from the base in an emergency or to respond to suspicious activity – another small window.

Finally, Art and Goose packed up the few items they had brought along for the stakeout and headed to the ground floor. At the appointed time, a car with Longwei in the driver's seat pulled up. Three steps from the building and they were in the back seat. Once the car door shut, Longwei gunned the engine and began to speed off at more than a reasonable speed. Art snapped at him, "Damnit Long, not so fast!"

Longwei, first with a surprised look and then a smile said, "Ok, sorry Art, I just wanting to have some fun! Been

cooped up like rooster in a cage and wanta crow a little."
He took his last, fast, corner followed by a rooster crow.
Long fancied himself as the best stunt car driver. His skills
were significant for both stunts and black operations, but
sometimes he slipped into stunt mode because it was more
entertaining.

Art, "I get that, but time for that will be after. Are you
gonna be able to wait a few more days, 'Rooster'?"

Longwei, "Sure Art, Rooster can wait, but gonna be a
rowdy time then! Much to celebrate when we take these
dudes down, huh?"

Art, "Yes, much to celebrate – when – we take these
guys down."

After that Longwei remained silent and drove calmly
focusing on getting Art back to the rendezvous at the hotel
by taking as few main streets as possible. A stunt driver by
trade, he loved to drive. In fact, Longwei was most
comfortable behind the wheel of a car, any car, than almost
anything else he could be doing. Black ops just served to
finance his passion for fast cars.

JIAGUO AND GAN
FREEDOM BAR SPIES

Jiaguo and Gan took the task of the Freedom Bar manufacturing facility in Shanghai. The plant was located in one of many industrial areas of the city. It was comprised of three main buildings where the processing, manufacture, and packaging of several 'power bar' like products took place. The main offices and security were located in the largest building which Jiaguo labeled as building "A". They noted that a group of vagrants showed up each day and hung out around a set of dumpsters next to the building they labeled "B". Jiaguo and Gan decided they needed a way to find out which building was making the "Freedom" bars. The vagrants were ignored by security and just the ticket for their intel gathering.

Gan dressed down in some tattered clothes and wandered in with the crowd of vagrants the next morning. Once inside he quietly moved between the buildings A, B, and C's loading docks and was followed by another member of the crowd of scavengers. *Hm*, he thought, *I have a puppy following me. Better to be careful.* So he continued, shuffling his feet and hunching over slightly to appear to be infirmed. It did not hurt that he had a scar on his left cheek that seemed to support his less fortunate image.

On his travels around the loading docks, he found that the crates and boxes being loaded out of buildings A and B were covered with brand name signage and markings, none of which were the target 'Freedom' bars. However, the crates being loaded from building C were unmarked. They would have to note that the primary target was building C.

Eventually, Gan and his 'puppy' were challenged by a security guard and Gan profusely begged forgiveness and asked for a handout for him and his puppy. The guard ushered them back to the crowd by the dumpster and then proceeded to enter building B. A moment later he came out with a carton containing a variety of snack packages, which to Gan's surprise, he handed out to the crowd before demanding they leave immediately. Fortunately, these were not labeled as the 'Freedom' bars, but Gan took no chance and simply left the crowd as he exited and returned to the place where Jiaguo was waiting.

Gan, "The Freedom bars maybe are processed in building C. I saw cartons and crates from building A and B that had labels with brand names and marks, but ones being loaded out of C were blank except for something like serial or asset numbers."

Jiaguo, "That's good to know, but I don't think Art and Da will want to take chance on targeting one building. Pretty sure whole place needs flattened."

Gan, "Agreed. We will need big bombs for this."

Jiaguo, "Indeed, but we have made some very big bombs in the past, you and me." he said with a smile.

Gan, "Yes, we have! Remember Pakistan Afghan border war in 2027? I think we brought down whole mountain!"

Jiaguo, "Ah, yes indeed that is one I remember. Too bad, there are no tunnels under this plant – are there?"

Gan, "We should ask Da, as he would be able to find out. Call him now."

With that, Jiaguo removed a small device from his boot and then attached another device from his backpack to it before adding one last piece to complete his encrypted disposable phone. He dialed the number for Da's disposable.

Jiaguo, "Uncle! Sammy and I are having good time in Shanghai and enjoying your recommendations."

Da, "Excellent. Are you finding everything you need?"

Jiaguo, "Yes indeed Uncle, but we were wondering if there are caves or tunnels in area beneath us, we love to explore dark places looking for our kind of excitement."

Da was well aware of their past escapades and knew immediately that he was asking about underground access to the plant area and buildings, "I am unaware of such sights and not thinking that an area so close to water will have such things, but I will research and let you know next time we meet."

Jiaguo, "Yes Uncle, I suppose you are correct about the water. Thank you so much, Uncle. See you soon."

With that, they disconnected the call and Jiaguo disassembled his phone, which disconnected the power source and rendered it un-traceable.

Jiaguo, "He will investigate for us and have a result when we meet. Any ideas?"

Gan, "Above ground seems very easy there is bad physical security and bad fence. We could just drive in a truck bomb."

Jiaguo, "Yes indeed, but to be complete we would need several. And to be complete the explosions must be very large. No one will want to be close to this plant when that happens."

Gan, "Very true."

Jiaguo, "There are many trucks parked at the buildings and they sit at loading areas waiting for loading or unloading. Maybe we can bring in many trucks late and leave them parked for the next day."

Gan, "Only, they won't be there next day!"

"Yes indeed." Jiaguo said softly, "Yes indeed."

WHAM AND LIGHTNIN'
BOTTLING PLANT RECON

Wham and Lightnin' headed for the water bottling and packaging plant in the port city of Tianjin. The plant was situated at the edge of a large industrial area. They set up shop in an abandoned grain storage facility that was scheduled to be demolished in three weeks to make space for a new warehouse complex. Some of the grain silos had a small shack at the top, which allowed the pair to get a bird's eye view of the area and a very good look at the bottling plant.

Behind them ran a river channel that several small boats used during the day to ferry barges back and forth from a scrap metal yard 1/2 kilometer to the west of their location. Beyond the river were a major roadway and several hundred kilometers beyond that, the beginning of normal residential areas – mainly one and two-story worker houses. The taller buildings of the port city were more than a kilometer and a half away. All of this was vital to the plan as the destruction of the bottling plant might involve collateral damage and they would want to minimize that. The point of their mission, after all, was to stop the wanton killing of innocent

Chinese, so as little collateral damage as possible would be one of their goals.

They monitored the comings and goings of the people working in the bottling plant and surrounding industries. Further away, the actual port area with its dock and piers was active around the clock, but in the immediate area around the bottling plant, the workers stuck to one long shift per day. All of the facilities were running one 16 hour shift per day from 5 AM to 10 PM with one lunch break in the early afternoon. During the lunch break, they noted that food trucks would appear outside the area of several facilities and provide meals to the workers. They also noted that workers from surrounding plants would flock to the food trucks, so on day two Wham headed down to the trucks to grab some lunch for him and Lightnin' and talk with the workers.

While waiting to get some food from one of the trucks Wham spotted an older gentleman that stood hunched over and moved very slowly. He helped the man with his lunch order and the two of them sat on a makeshift bench assembled from old pallets. He learned that the old man had worked at the bottling plant since it opened some 15 years prior and that it was hard work, but the pay was good and his job was not too strenuous. He was known as the Label Man and his job was to monitor a machine that wrapped the labels around the bottles. When the big roll of labels was running low, he would lift the fresh 10-kilogram rolls onto a spindle and the machine would spit the spent roll tube out and take the new roll while it continued non-stop.

For the Label Man, this was the hardest part of the job – lifting the 10-kilo roll onto the spindle which happened about once every 15 minutes. Wham asked about the shift work and the old man confirmed that the plant emptied out by 10 PM daily, giving the workers just enough time to get home, have a meal, and get some rest. This was the man's livelihood and he performed the same routine every single day to provide for his family. Wham felt a pang of guilt knowing that he was going to be responsible for taking the man's purpose and income from him, but for the good of the many - it was a necessary evil.

In the conversation, he asked about the people that worked past 10 PM and the old man offered that there were a few security and maintenance people that worked in the after-hours. They were there to fix any broken machines and make sure the regular maintenance was performed to keep the machines running like a clock. Wham thanked the man once their lunch was over and the old man wished Wham good fortune in his work. Wham could only smile a half-smile as he waved by to the man. Perhaps when the mission was done, he would send a gift to the old man. Wham had more money than he could ever use, so he took a selfie of himself and the old man. Goose would be able to do the biometrics and get the name of the old man and where he lived.

Later, Wham and Lightnin' would note one security guard in particular who always took a smoke break at 2 AM outside a door on the south side of the building about midway down its length. They observed a total of six security personnel with four on staff during the day and two arriving before 10 PM for a shift change, leaving only the pair through the night. It seemed that the plant needed six guards during the start and end of each workday and only two that stayed the night when no workers, save for the maintenance people, were on site. They knew this would allow them to minimize human carnage while inflicting unavoidable collateral damage to surrounding buildings.

The bottling complex itself was large and the bottling building stretched just over 100 meters in length. Trucks from many different trucking companies, some without distinct markings, were lined up several rows deep on each side of the building. They were queued for loading of outgoing products and incoming raw materials and packaging and were left unattended for long periods. Hiding a few trucks in plain sight would not be a problem. If they went this route they could call in a bomb threat and possibly evacuate the remaining people in the building and maybe save a couple of additional lives. That would be a decision left for the final planning, but it was noted for their report to the group.

Wham remarked, "With Da's expertise we should be able to secure many trucks and fake incoming supply deliveries for the plant, then park trucks and wait till after hours to blow them remotely."

Lightin' agreed, "Yea, seems pretty ok. Of course, we'll be having backup for the triggers to ensure they go even if remotes are not able to communicate."

To which Wham added, "Yeah, plan B, C, and D since no one will want to be close to this place when it goes. What ya think? Semtex?"

"Na," replied Lightnin', "ammonium nitrate and diesel fuel since we have ability to set many trucks. Take out whole place and some of its neighbors too."

"Oh yeah," said Wham, "Whadda ya think bout adding in some magnesium powder like in fireworks?"

"That mean Wham, just plain mean," said Lightnin' smiling, "we just want to take out plant and not whole city!"

Wham ended with, "I do like me some big fireworks."

Several times during the three days, they walked past the plant taking video of the entrance and perimeter fencing before casually grabbing lunch. The fence was poorly maintained and not secure. It was not topped with any kind of human deterrent and there were stray cats and dogs all over the property. The fence was like Swiss cheese with the number of holes in it.

They sketched out the area and their ideas along with notes on the location of surveillance cameras they could find. When they completed their work they grabbed a train and headed back to the hotel to meet up with the rest of the team.

DA, DESHI, AND DINGBANG
SEEKING FRIED RICE

Da, Deshi, and Dingbang set out for the rice fields located near Yiyang in the province of Hunan. Hunan is a province in China known for its rice production. It is also known for its large markets, and Yiyang was no exception. Even though the city was relatively small the men were able to mingle at the markets and gather intel to help narrow down the location of the specific field or fields to target without fear of discovery.

Da and his team got help from Joshua and Dave Tillis using clandestine phone surveillance and a specifically positioned and tasked satellite to further narrow the possible target location. Josh and Dave were able to identify the location of a recently harvested field in an area just south-southwest of the city center. The satellite image provided by the NSA was excellent. The image was transmitted to Da's phone and the team on the ground reviewed it carefully.

With the image in hand Da and his team were back to the markets to gather more data on the potential target. They were able to confirm that the field Josh and Dave had identified was indeed the target and appeared to be a secured compound. Locals commented on the commotion around the rice field a few months ago and that the area was now off-limits and fenced.

Deshi hiked in from the south and was able to get a good view from up in a tall tree. He confirmed that an area of the compound contained solar panels and there was one clean building on the grounds. There was a water pond to the south and, of course, the complete perimeter of trees blocking the view of the property. He also noted a security patrol and only one apparent entrance to the north of the fields containing rows of rice plants.

He photographed the guard's weapons. Each guard, while on patrol, carried an AK-47 style rifle affixed with a bayonet, a sidearm, and a baton. They were serious about the protection of the facility. The crop sprayer would have one or two passes that might be uninterrupted, but eventually, the guards would surely notice and engage the threat. Soo Lin would need to be very aware of this as it is unlikely her plane would able to defend itself considering its low altitude being an easy target for even an unskilled marksman using an AK.

Deshi noted that it might be wise to station a volunteer with a sniper-style weapon and the correct protective gear to assist in threat protection against the armed guards. His observation spot in the trees was not a bad location and with a night vision scope, the guards would initially be easy prey. Of course, when the shooting started the muzzle flash would be a dead giveaway, possibly lethal, but there would be confusion amongst the guards at first and that might be the extra edge needed to accomplish the task of spraying the field and providing cover fire for the pilot.

Based on their observations and estimates the fields covered an area roughly 600 meters west to east and 750 meters north to south. This information combined with Deshi's notes and the satellite image would assist Soo Lin in her plan to spray the rice crop and the team's ability to accomplish its goal with this facility. Once they completed photographing the areas they could access without being observed, they compiled their notes and headed to a rendezvous with the entire team.

MEETING OF THE MINDS
OPERATION – DRAGON DOWN

After the three days of recon the team was again gathered at the Wuhan 'hotel', previously designated to discuss their findings and formulate a plan and timeline. As he had before, Da swept the room for bugs and hidden microphones or cameras before giving the all-clear. This time, Soo Lin was present at the start of the meeting and smiling at Art, but remained silent while mentally reveling over the cute joke that she and Da played on him a few days earlier. Art began with the overall objectives.

Art, "Before we go over the recon results I want to emphasize that our primary objective is to eradicate the virus and the current means of distribution. We need to get all traces of the virus removed regardless of the medium it occupies. We can leave no formula or trace evidence for the Chinese government to resurrect this heinous weapon to be used in any country again. Secondly, we will be helping to protect the Chinese people from being targeted by this weapon and prevent it from being sold to other governments around the world. Our only mission is to stop this particular assault and do so with the grandest, most in your face, message we can manage. Bigger is better and will make a statement the 'dishonorable' Chairman will not be able to ignore. Is that clear?"

All present, except for Goose who blinked once, nodded with some members of the group chiming in with "Yes" and "Here, here". Art made his point that this part of his mission, the part he was expecting to engage in with this team, was about the greater good and punching the Chinese government's Dragon in the face. No one in the group could deny this was a noble cause and necessary at all costs. It would help eliminate a great threat to the safety and lives of many Chinese people, but also, people of the world. They knew their small team would be the unsung heroes whose names would not be known and whose effort might be construed by others as terrorism.

Art then had Goose project satellite images onto a fairly clean and somewhat whitish looking wall.

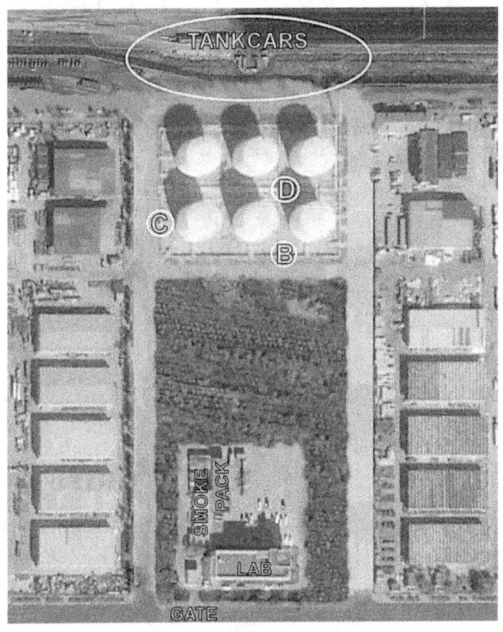

Art then began his briefing of their observations, "From what my buddy, Goose, and I observed, the lab in Dongguan appears to have been built in an unfortunate location."

Goose,

Webster: Buddy: FRIEND sense 1

Webster: Friend: one attached to another by affection or esteem

Goose blinked once. If he could have smiled he would have a big smile now.

Art continuing, "The lab sits on a fairly level piece of ground with a berm, possibly for security purposes, on the south end where the main entrance is located. It has a three-meter fence around the perimeter topped with razor wire. Above the lab and further to the north is a tank farm with a grove of trees between the tanks and the lab."

While Art spoke, Goose shared some of the videos he'd stored with the team via their smartphones and his local Wi-Fi VPN. The team could follow Art's discussion and the projected satellite image while seeing the video details Goose was sharing, synchronized with the areas Art covered in his discussion. "From what I know of Chinese writing, it appears these tanks hold fuel."

At that point, Goose zoomed the video to enlarge the Chinese writing on the tanks, and Da spoke up. "Yes, Art. These tanks hold diesel fuel for transportation vehicles."

Art continued, "Thanks Da, I was pretty sure it was something flammable and able to flow downhill. It's almost too good to be true, but I did not see anything in the last three days that would indicate we should avoid using these fuel tanks. Goose and I noted the railroad tank cars come and go above the fuel tanks and we were not sure, initially, if they were loading or unloading. That is until Goose zoomed in on one of them and noted the springs on the tank car trucks were more compressed when the cars arrived than when they left. It certainly appears that they are offloading to the tanks. I think it gives us just that much more fuel to dump on the lab."

Jake interrupted, "About how much fuel?"

Art, "Well, Goose and I figured the tanks hold about 210,000 gallons and the tank cars maybe 25,000 gallons. Goose how much is that in liters?"

Goose, `"Fuel tank 800,000 liters. Tank car 94,500 liters."`

Art, "Thanks Goose."

Goose blinks once.

Art, "That's a few million liters if the tanks are full. What do you think Jake? Is that enough for a fire?"

Jake, "Aye, we can roast a few bangers on a fire like that — not that I want to be anywhere near there when it happens. Of course, that depends on our mission not getting rained out."

Goose, `"Checking meteorological. No rain forecast."`

Art, "Ok then. So, we observed that the facility staff comes in the AM and is out by nightfall with one or two guards remaining to spend the night. Two vans are left on the property at night and are in and out of the facility several times each day. I had Longwei follow both vans to see if they traveled the same routes in case we might need to intercept one. Long, what do you have for me on that?"

Longwei, "Both vans travel to various places picking up items or supplies mostly, but with some drop deliveries. Some of the stops are the same, but never same time each day except for one daily trip. The one van is driven by a man in a business suit wearing a tie. He drives 3.4 kilometers to small house near Shijing Road. House is at end of the complex and borders Fengjing golf course. This house has wall surrounding it and tennis court. He is greeted by very beautiful young woman and not seen again until he leaves house. He spends from 45 minutes to over one hour with woman. Not sure who woman is, but he has his own car and choose to use lab van for this one trip each time. We could have access to van while at this location."

Art, "Longwei, thank you. Job well done. So, any ideas on how we can take the lab out?"

Da spoke up first, "What ideas do you have Art?"

Art, "Thanks, Da. I am thinking we use the fuel tanks and dump a river of the stuff on the lab property. We can add in some more fuel from the tank cars as that should flow down to the lab as well."

Jimbo jumps in here saying, "I vote for the extra fuel since you want a BIG fire. Can't have too much flammable material now, can we?"

To which Art responded, "Thanks Jimbo, I was trying to leave it as an option, but I like your reasoning. We'll need a few extra bodies to manage those tank cars. Probably three guys, can you arrange for that Da?"

Da, "No problem. I can get you all the Chinese patriots you need and many very talented people."

Art continued, "So we have to deal with video surveillance of the area, and I suspect that will be an issue with the other locations. I'll see what my guys at home can do on that and let you all know if we can manage a large scale outage. As a contingency, for the lab, Goose located a communications box on the west side of the tank farm, just off the road heading south. It's where he was able to tap into the State-run surveillance camera feeds. We should be able to just run the thing down and temporarily shut down the cameras.

And that leaves the security patrols that drive by at 15 minutes before the hour. They are always in and out of the immediate lab area in a few minutes and then off to other areas to the west. We did not see them again until the next patrol an hour later. So, we got a window from when they leave to when they could make it back to the area. I figure if they drive for 12 to 15 minutes then the lights go out, they might be tasked to return if the authorities can quickly identify the problem. That would give us about 10 minutes to breach the retaining wall and open the supply pipe. The tank car thing can happen in parallel - same time frame. We're talking about getting into position, lugging tools over the wall, placing charges to take out the wall, detonation of the charges, and opening the wall. At the same time a couple of guys to disconnect a 10" pipe elbow with 40 bolts total and finally opening the valve to release the fuel. Thoughts?"

Longwei chimed in first, "I got a couple of guys I know that can handle the pipe thing. They are like guys in your American Indy 500 pit crew – very, very fast with tools. 20 bolts each should take one to two minutes total. Of course, they might want to carry fitting home with them." He ended that comment with a smile.

Art, "That's fine Longwei, but let's make sure we don't involve too many civilians in a black op ok?"

Da, "I can supply battery-operated tools and a lightweight blast blanket. What about the charges?"

Jake jumped in, "A couple of shaped charges fastened to the wall with a couple of support arms anchored in the ground – no worries. I can make them light enough to carry in a couple of average suitcases. I'd use me a concrete nail gun to attach to the wall and a couple of screw in-ground anchors. Should take about five minutes to set up and blast it. I can keep it simple so that all you'll hear will be a wee thump. One and done, so to speak."

Jimbo and Wham nodded in agreement while Lightnin' sat quietly, not showing approval or disapproval.

Art, "Any other input?"

Feng spoke up, "We can send one of us Shi along to keep watch and help in case there is trouble."

Art, "Thanks Feng it would be good to have extra security just in case we need a few more minutes. The goal is to keep this as silent as we can so there is no interference until after the place is in flames and get out undetected."

Jake, "So, how do we ignite this lake of fuel?"

Art, "Yeah, almost forgot that little detail, do you have a plan?"

Jake, 'We could stake a device in the ground and ensure it is placed into the flow of the fuel spill, or we got the van guy, so why not place an incendiary under the van someplace inconspicuous, like next to the gas tank? You know, with a remote trigger and failsafe, just in case. That would put the source of ignition at the target instead of above it. Of course, someone would have to be near enough to set it off and be sure it did the job."

Jimbo nodded and added his approval, "I like the van idea, cause it makes sure the river of fuel is at the lab before it's ignited. That should keep more fuel pouring in before the fire tracks back to the tank farm. We don't need to risk a back burn and send the fire back to the source rather than down to the facility. Besides, putting a charge in the flow might be a risk to proper detonation."

Jake, a little miffed at the resistance to his idea, "I like the van idea, but I could handle the device being in the fuel. I have a wee bit of experience in that technique."

Gan, "Sure, the van, and with a backup plan. Maybe, a sniper rifle with phosphorus tracers just in case remote does not do job."

Art, "I knew we had the right guys to plan this. The van it is. With someone stationed in the building that Goose and I used for the stakeout, to pull the trigger on the van and tracer rounds for backup - so far, so good. One last thing, I want all of these separate facilities to go down at the same time. Exactly would be nice, but within minutes of each other so that there is no chance the authorities will have time to pick up on what's happening and possibly save one or more of these places. We'll consider timing once the rest of the team has presented their recon info and ideas." Art looked over at Soo Lin for a moment and without taking his eyes off of her he said, "Da, why don't you go next with your intel on the rice production."

Art stepped to the side to allow Da to share his team's intel. Da stepped up and handed out a few printed pages of the sat photo he had gotten from Joshua in the U.S. while Goose projected it on the wall.

Then he began, "We received this satellite photo from our U.S. friends. They had been tracking phone calls by Dr. Yīshēng and that led them to this possible target which appeared to have rice paddies. Deshi, Dingbang, and I hung out with the locals at markets and confirm there was an old rice field there and many months ago there was much activity in that area. The Chinese military added a fence to perimeter, a building, a water pond, and solar panel." He looked at Soo and then said, "They also added armed soldiers to guard property."

Before he could continue, Soo Lin spoke up, "Oh great, I gotta fly at night, over trees, 20 meters off ground and get SHOT AT!" Which, she followed with a few choice Chinese swear words equivalent to the English f-word - and worse.

Goose, fluent in Chinese and Mandarin began to translate, but Da interrupted. "Yes, well, it gets better for you. We will need to eliminate the building as well, so that means you will carry the chemical for the rice, fuel for the plane, and a bomb to drop before you can be done. But, it is good that there are no power wires over the field."

Soo Lin was even more pissed and Da wisely backed up partly hiding behind Art. She was cussing up a blue streak and shaking her fists and even stomping the floor frantically. If there had been any heavy objects to throw, she would have done that as well.

Art spoke up, loudly, at first, and then more quietly, "Soo Lin, calm down! You are going to wake the neighbors and draw attention to us."

Goose quietly sat observing Soo Lin, her words did not match her biometrics and Goose knew that she was about to make humor at Art's expense again – One blink to Soo.

And Art continued, "Calm down. If you want I'll fly with you and try to provide some cover by shooting back." He was desperate to shut her down and avoid the risk of blowing their cover.

Soo Lin did settle a bit and then looked at Art and said, in a very matter-of-fact manner, "You not gonna fit you big American ass in my tiny plane. I gotta have room for chemicals and a bomb. Besides I been through worse than this. I had a mother-in-law once - she was Korean! Boy, talk about being shot at."

Soo Lin continued with erotic sounding oohs and aahs of passion escalating in volume, along with some raunchy twerking for a false lovefest. She whispered to Art, "Make up sex sweetie. Just a sample."

With that, she smiled a big smile and knew she had gotten Art again. Da, still hiding behind Art, chuckled as well, but she had gotten him just a good. Art thought about saying something regarding the seriousness of the matter before them and the need to dispense with the humor. He held back knowing that the work they were doing was incredibly stressful so a little levity was probably a good thing.

Da stepped out from behind Art and asked, "Any ideas on the armed soldiers?"

Jiaguo said, "You got many trees around this area. How many armed soldiers are on property at night?"

Da responded, "We counted four at any time except when changing guards was happening, but that was only in daylight."

Jiaguo continued, "We put sniper in the tree with protective gear, chemical mask, and night vision. He takes out soldiers - is very easy. They be confused at first and not shooting – probably. Sniper would have four easy targets and quick to reduce threat or draw fire from Soo."

Soo Lin walked over to Jiaguo, who stood motionless while leaning on a table along the wall behind him. She wrapped one of her tiny arms around his waist and, while facing the group, said, "I like this guy lotso! Be careful Mr. Art American, you might let Miss Hot Soo Lin slip away from you." Then looking at Da said, "Can I have a sniper?"

Art now blushing again, responded, "Jiaguo, if you are ok with that then it's a go for the sniper overwatch."

Jiaguo, "No problem."

Da, "Thanks Jiaguo, we will get the gear for you and arrange for extraction." Then he continued, "We saw one field of rice harvested. It went into the building and one day later was loaded on a truck. Dingbang followed the truck for many miles heading to Shanghai. He added a tracker when truck stopped for fuel. The U.S. friends told me the truck went to the factory in Shanghai where the 'Freedom' bars are made."

Gan interrupted, "Yes, we saw trucks of rice come in and many trucks with rice go out. Very confusing cause we thought rice comes in and bars go out, but rice comes in and bars AND bags of rice go out."

Art, "Yes, my Savior Unit friends in the U.S., that's what they call themselves, tell me that the sacks of rice they have intercepted have only a portion of the rice contaminated with virus spores. It looks like the 'Freedom' bar factory mixes the modified rice with good rice, then splits part of the mixed rice into sacks for export to the U.S. and some into 'Freedom' bars. Da, did you see any other trucks leaving with rice?"

Da, "No, only the one crop was picked, and one truck leaving in those three days."

Art, "Da or anyone have more on the rice facility?"

Da, "No, that is all we have for you."

Hungqu, who had remained quiet thus far, had a question, "Do we know where rice goes from 'Freedom' bar factory?"

Art, "That's a good question. I know that some or all of it is being exported to the U.S., but I am not sure if any goes somewhere else. We'll need to get some eyes to track those trucks leaving the 'Freedom' bar facility and see where they go."

Duyi, "I can do that while others are preparing the fun time."

Art, "Excellent Duyi, thanks. Since we are talking about the rice and 'Freedom' bars I'd like Jiaguo and Gan to go next and tell us what they found."

Neither Jiaguo nor Gan moved from their seats. Gan placed two sketches on the coffee table in front of the munitions guys. Again, Goose projected a marked up sat image on the wall.

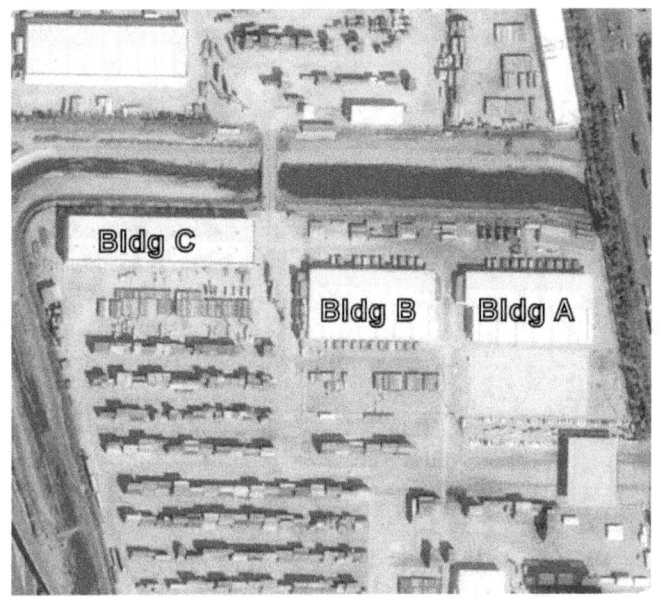

Jiaguo then began, "There are three buildings at the factory. They have workers in the factory from 5 AM to 10 PM. Then only two security guards after 10. The factory has fence, but fence is shit. Gan was able to get close to the buildings and find buildings A and B have shipping boxes with labels of real things. Building C boxes have no labels and this where rice comes in then rice bags and bars go out."

Gan stepped in now, "There are many trucks at the factory. Many trucks coming in and many trucks going out and many trucks stay overnight and some trucks did not move for the three days we watched. Some trucks come late at night before workers leave and wait for next day to be unloaded or loaded. Some of these trucks park at loading docks overnight. Always this happens when the truck come in late. It would be good to bring truck bombs in late at night."

Jake, "So you two think truck bombs are the way to go and we just hide them in plain sight? Makes sense since we don't have a fuel storage facility next to the plant. I can support this Art."

Art, "Ok, so we might have the start of something here. What else do we know Gan?"

Gan, "There are cameras around the factory and other factories nearby. Worker houses are over more than one kilometer away. We think all the factories nearby have same worker shift from 5 AM to 10 PM because we see big crowds come in at 5 AM and leave at 10 PM and no other crowds at other times.

Jake, "So we set things up to go boom between 10 PM and 5 AM and we should minimize human casualties."

At that point, the room went dead silent. Even though Art had mentioned people working at the lab, no one in the room connected the takedowns to the possibility of the loss of lives except for the armed military threats. Soo Lin, in particular, had a feeling of dread wash over her – one the likes of which she had not felt for many years. People, innocent people, were going to die. She said in a whisper, "I don't like this."

Art, "Alright, I thought it was clear that this was not easy and we were going to be saving countless lives by taking out the facilities making and using this virus. You guys need to know that over 12 million U.S. citizens died from this shit before we could stop it. I saw that happen. That's happening here now and will be much bigger. If the Chinese government succeeds in its plan to use this, we'll see 100's of millions of people around the world die horrible deaths. Could be some of your friends or family. This virus stuff, this would make the Devil himself cringe. Goose, show me some of the autopsy stuff." Goose did as instructed and pulled up one of the autopsy images showing the internal damages caused by the virus.

Art continued, "We are all patriots here. We might be

brothers and sister from different mothers, but we are all here for the greater good and to stop this evil thing from continuing. Yes, there will be casualties, and yes some of those will be innocent victims caught in our little war. And, yes, some of us might not make it. If anyone wants out the time is now because we cannot slow down, we cannot get soft, we cannot fail. I need you all to tell me you are on board and will see this through."

One by one the room's occupants responded in the affirmative. Even Goose blinked once confirming his commitment. Soo Lin was last and apologized, "I am sorry Art. I have been through worse and will die for this mission if I got too, but I forgot about people who might suffer or die." And then, after a pause, "I am ok."

Art, "Thank you Soo, and thank you all. As I said, I have seen what this stuff does to people. They get this and they suffer and die from all kinds of things and none of that is a quick or easy death. Glad you are all with me on this and trust me, it is a greater cause than you may have ever fought for in the past."

Art, "Gan and Jiaguo, any more we should know before moving on to the final target?"

Jiaguo, "We did not see any security patrols as you saw around the lab. Security around the factory was very lax."

Gan, "Agreed, they do not care about the scavengers on the property, and security only come to me when I was close to building C. He just move me back to dumpsters where scavengers were. I think we cover it all."

Jiaguo, "Indeed."

Art, "That leaves Wham and Lightnin'. What did you guys observe?"

Wham stood to point out areas on the image of the bottling plant that Goose was showing on the wall.

Lightnin' started to share their intel with the group. "The plant is located in the city of Tianjin, near the actual port area. The plant and several industries are about 1/2 kilometer from the docks and piers of the shipping port. We were up high to observe from row of abandoned grain silos sitting between river channel and bottling plant to north.

Like 'Freedom' bar factory, industrial area has one shift from 5 AM to 10 PM, but ports are active all day and night. Workers at factory come at 5 AM and leave at 10 PM. There are several security guards on-site at all time and they do patrols. Patrols are not set and seem to be random, but we could not see into building. At night there are only two guards. There are few maintenance workers at night also. They fix and get machines ready for next day. A worker told me they work seven days a week like this.

As with the 'Freedom' bar factory, bottling plant has lots of trucks parked. Trucks are parked along sides of building in rows until they move to loading and unloading areas when needed."

Jake chimed in, "Seems a wee bit too easy. Like the luck o' the Irish."

Art then interjected, "Yeah, well, that still would mean we gotta pull together a lot of truck bombs and get them to two different places and coordinate getting them there late and passing through the security guards and then ensuring they are not opened until the next day and get the drivers, our people, out of there, so, not that easy."

Jake, "Well, I was talkin about making the bombs."

Wham, added, "Lightnin' and I are thinking ammonium nitrate, diesel fuel, and maybe some magnesium power like they use in fireworks!"

Lightnin', "Calm down Whamo, don't jump outta your shorts." Then followed with, "But, I am down with dat!"

To which Jake responded with a smile, "I like the way you guys think."

Art, "Wham and Lightnin', continue please."

Lightnin', "We walked the perimeter a few times and I..." he paused to flip through the notes on his phone, "I don't see fence in my notes, but fence was pretty new and still shiny. Typical perimeter fence look about three meters tall with barbed wire of some kind at top. No holes a few locked gates outside of the main entrance. That about it. We are just thinking big truck bombs spread out around building, maybe two or three each side of building. If we put them on inside, between rows of trucks and building, then we'd get a little help to push blasts in to the building. From both sides, we think it flattens the place."

Jake, "Yeah. We could add some interior structure to the truck container to help that some as well."

Art, "Anything else on the bottling facility?" Both Wham and Lightnin' were shaking their heads indicating a 'no'. So Art continued, "Alright, so we have the intel and ideas for the methods and devices we need. Let's talk timing. Da, how fast can you get the trucks and chemicals we need?"

Da, "Depends how much chemical and where you need it delivered. Maybe three days."

Art, "Da, we'll need a bomb-making location somewhere between Tianjin and Shanghai. Also, I'll need a list of material from you bomb makers and fast."

Jake, looking at the other guys, "We should be able to have a list with quantities in a couple of hours. We're going to need lots of ammonium nitrate and some magnesium powder. Diesel won't be a problem. Then we need some detonators, power sources, remotes and lots of wire." The three other munitions guys were nodding their agreement.

Da, "I can do these things once list is complete. I still stick by three days."

Art, "Da, I'm gonna hold you to that. Guys, how long to build out the explosives and have everything ready to deploy?"

Jake again led the response, "At least two days and probably three, but depends on how much help we have to build out these. Going to be filling a lot of barrels and a lot of wiring. There are four of us, but maybe three or four more bodies?" Again, the other munitions guys nodded approval of the estimate.

Art, "Then we set a date seven days from today. Which gives us three days to get materials and three days to build out the bombs and trucks. Leaving us one day to get the trucks in place. Da, I trust you can pull in as much manpower as we need to assist with the bomb-making? But remember that every person outside this room is a potential security risk to the mission."

Da, "Yes, there is no shortage of Chinese willing to help for a price – I got this."

Art, "Good. Soo Lin, Are you set with getting a plane to do the crop spraying?"

Soo Lin, "Yes, no problem."

Art, "The last thing is the time of day and I am thinking after midnight – something like zero hour is 2 AM, one week from today. Thoughts?"

None of the team members expressed an issue with 2 AM as zero hour.

Art, "Any more questions or ideas?" The team members all nodded or mumbled a 'no' response. "Good. I'd like Da and the munitions guys to hang back here to get our list of supplies together. The rest of you can stay or leave and we'll meet back here in the morning to sync up. Again, thank you all for your contributions. We are going to save a great many lives despite the damage we will cause. There will be no recognition, but that of your teammates and a few folks helping us from the U.S. I want you all to know that I have trust and faith in all of you and I am proud to be working with this team. Finally, if you think of anything, and I mean any little detail we might have overlooked or is a concern to you, please let us know ASAP.

Soo, I have that other mission for you if you are done being angry with me. Goose and I are going to be heading to Beijing before the final op, to do a small job involving the disappearance of a private jet and Doctor Yīshēng. If you don't want the second mission, I'll ask the rest of the team to assist in getting another pilot. This mission is to get rid of a stash of the virus and dispatch Doctor Yīshēng who is the main player in the plan to kill off the freedom demonstrators and the many incarcerated in the camps."

Art had barely finished the sentence when Soo responded with, "Details handsome, don't make me cane your big American ass." So he furnished details, as demanded, not knowing if she was serious about caning.

Dai would need to fly to Beijing in advance for his part of that mission. Goose and Art would also as they had a little swap to perform. Soo would meet the Doctor in Beijing, impersonate his pilot and get him and his droid to Stephanie's plane, and then help with the droid stuff, and getting the plane off the ground – without being compromised.

PREPARATIONS
PARTING OF THE WAYS

The next morning the team gathered in Art and Goose's room for a final checkpoint meeting. Art began, "Alright, Da has the list of materials needed and has identified a rural area outside Jining which is about eight hours' drive to either Tianjin or Shanghai. There we will split the munitions guys into two teams. Jake and Jimbo, you'll lead one team with Wham and Lightnin' leading the other. We don't want all our eggs in one basket, so to speak."

Jake interrupted at that point having felt a bit of his pride eroding, "Are you insinuating that one of us four might botch this and blow ourselves up!?!."

Art replied, "Uh, not exactly, but you never know. I mean we are dealing with explosives here and I can't risk the mission on one tiny mishap."

To which Jake shot back, "We're not a bunch of efin eejits or fluthered suicide vest makers here. We are trained AND seasoned experts in our line of work!"

Art, "Yes, Jake and I have the highest regard for your work having seen the results many times, but you asked for some helpers and…"

Jake, "Oh, yeah, there is that wee bit. Sorry Art, I'll shut up now."

Art, "No problem. As I was saying, the munitions guys will be in two teams at a couple of farms about 3.5 kilometers apart. Da has asked that you do not communicate with each other and that you send all communications through him. We will be using code words for the team so remember these for when you need to communicate. Da, the code words for the bomb makers, please."

Da, "Jake and Jimbo, you will be Dragon's Breath and Wha and Lightnin' you will be Hell-Fire. Any questions?"

Jake responded, "Ah, what do we call you?"

Da, "I am Uncle."

Soo Lin popped in now, "What's my code name?"

To which Da responded, "You are Momma."

Soo Lin, "Momma? You kidding? Do I look like you Momma? You momma look fine as Soo, she shoulda done better than bring a horse-faced Da into world!" and she spat on the floor. But just in case she hadn't made her point already, she sauntered to Art's side and looked sweetly up and said, "Uncle Art, Soo will be your momma any ole time.", as she pushed her unfettered breasts against his arm. Again, she had made him blush.

Art was a little miffed, but remained composed and just a little loud when he continued, "OK! Now let's cut the crap with the code names. The two bomb-making locations need code names because there will be many people in two different locations, so they get code names. Da needs to know which team needs something and where it has to get to fast. Everybody else just use something related to your location if you need to communicate. Like; I need a bottle of water, I'm hungry for a power bar, I ordered some fried rice or I'm going to get tested at the lab. We'll sort it out from there." Then he looked at Soo Lin and said, "Da, you can refer to Soo Lin as 'Hot Momma' if you need her to have a code name." Then he smiled and Soo Lin smiled back. She was blushing. Art was thinking, *At long last, score one for Art.* Goose is learning and he blinked once.

Art again, "All right, so we got our material lists to Da and we have a location for the bomb-making. Da, have you started on the material list?"

Da, "Yes, I got people getting trucks. There will be twelve, and I got two mechanics will check each truck to avoid breakdowns. I have people collecting barrels, pallets, and straps. Fertilizer not there until tomorrow. Wire, detonators, batteries, and remotes also on way to locations. We are good to go on these items. I have person getting weapons and other gear we need for lab and rice facility. No problems so far."

Art, "Excellent work. Let me know if there are any snafus. Juyi you volunteered to stakeout the 'Freedom' bar factory and then follow the rice that leaves the place and let me know where it goes. I have to know where it goes. We gotta have a plan for that stuff if it is not going to the U.S."

Duyi, "Roger that."

Art, "I still need someone to get a device on that lab van. Hungqu, can I count on you to keep watch on the lab and get a device on the van and be our trigger guy?"

Hungqu, "Yes, I can do it. I will need device and instructions."

Jake, "I'll get that device built and Da will get it to you with instructions. It'll be simple to attach and have a simple remote trigger."

Hungqu, "Good, then no problem."

Art, "Feng, you suggested a Shi to provide over watch for the Lab, can I count on you to protect Da's crew doing the Lab fuel spill?"

Feng, "Very much, thank you." Feng bowed as he was honored to have the assignment.

Art bowed in return and continued, "So I'll need two volunteers to be the trigger guys for the two factories."

Jake spoke first, "I'd like the bottling plant and I'd want my trucks there as well. I like the location and would love to see my work through."

Art, "All righty then. That leaves the 'Freedom' bar factory in Shanghai. Any takers?"

Lightnin', "Wham and I will take that one. I have relatives about 10 klicks from there, so gotta place to lay low after."

Art, "Ok, if there are no questions then the guys that need to get moving now can head out. The rest of you sit tight until you're contacted – Da will be in touch. I know that most of you will be staying in China after this, so be careful and good luck. Jake and Jimbo, your exit is to the south via Yunnan province and your cover as nature documentary guys. Then you cross into Laos and you should be home free. Anything else?"

Wham spoke up, "Just that we will be ready if you need us again."

Jake and Jimbo added, "Here, here." With Jake continuing, "If we get through this we'll be waiting for your next mission!"

Art knew that most of the team was staying in China after, and had their respective local arrangements covered. They'd been involved in a few things in China before and were well-rehearsed with escape routes, cover stories, and alibies. They'd be fine.

Art, "Glad to hear it. I tell you all this, I got a place in Hawaii on the north shore of Kauai. It's on the beach at the end of the highway and you can't miss it. Let's all meet there a month from now." The whole team smiled and gave thumbs up to the suggestion.

Goose, `Can Goose meet on beach too?`

That drew chuckles and laughter from the team. Art responded, "Goose, buddy, you and I are sticking together for a long time!"

Goose, one blink.

Art, "Alright, you guys head out and the rest of you hang out. Soo, Wei, Goose, and I have a separate little mission to take care of. We have a doctor visit scheduled. If I don't get to see you here soon, then see you all in a month." With that, the team split up and headed out.

PREPARATIONS
MUNITIONS

The munitions teams split into two groups using separate vehicles. They would follow the same route together and then split up when they were near their destinations. Wham and Lightnin' were Asians so their cover was easy – they were visiting friends in another province, beyond their destination. Da rode with Jake and Jimbo with the two white guys using the cover of nature documentary videographers in search of the rare Snub-Nosed Monkey. They would say they were traveling to Yunnan province, which was beyond their intended destination as well.

The trip was uneventful and there was little conversation. At one point they encountered a military checkpoint. These were not uncommon in China and there were many permanent facilities one had to pass through unless one managed to find a back road or another way around them. However, some were randomly set up and temporary. This was one of the temporary checkpoints and not on Da's radar. Wham and Lightnin' had no issue passing through with their cover. Da, Jake, and Jimbo were not so lucky.

While Da and the guys were detained at the checkpoint, Wham and Lightnin' stopped a distance down the road where they could look back and see what was going on, in case they might need to intervene. The ranking officer of the guards at the checkpoint asked Da to pull over when he spotted the tall white male in the front seat with the bright carrot red hair. The guys got out of the car and Da proceeded to explain that he was their tour guide and assisting these gentlemen on their quest.

He explained that they were nature videographers and heading to Yunnan to see if they could capture video of the rare Snub-Nosed Monkey. The guard looked over their credentials and equipment and found nothing out of order. He was not concerned, but still, he had them wait while he went into the guard tent on the side of the road.

Da was getting nervous, but Jake was calm as could be thanks to his little birth defect. Seems when he was born there were issues with his amygdala. These tiny areas of the human brain affect certain perceptions, among other things. His were about 1/10 the normal size and impacted his ability to respond to fear stimuli. In other words, Jake was pretty much fearless, which in his current occupation, was a good thing. It led him to be calm and steady even when things were blowing up around him or bullets were whizzing overhead.

After a few minutes, which seemed like an eternity to Da, the guard exited the tent carrying a folded piece of paper and headed to the team waiting outside their car. He smiled and motioned for them to follow him to the hood where he unfolded a map. He began to explain where they were heading and pointed out a lake in the Yunnan province. He told Da, in Chinese, that he had been hiking to the north above Fuxian Lake near the village of Hiakouzhen in the surrounding mountains and had the honor of encountering several of the Snub-Nosed Monkeys they were seeking. He circled the area and wrote the name of the specific trail on the map. Da translated for Jake and Jimbo, who graciously smiled and thanked the man in English.

Da told the guard he was honored that the guard had shared his encounter and provided so much good information for them. He told the guard that this would help him be successful with his business and that the Englishmen would be very pleased as well. The men shook hands and bowed several times before climbing in their car and heading off to shouts of good luck from the guard. All was again as planned and the two teams were back on track to get to their destinations. No more checkpoints or hazards impeded them on the remainder of their trip.

Da, Jake, and Lightnin' arrived at their farm to find the trucks neatly parked under trees in a grove just off the side of a large wooden barn. Two men were already hard at work retrofitting the interiors with steel angle reinforcements from the sketch provided to Da the night before. Wood posts, which looked like used railroad ties, would be affixed to the right side of each trailer. Jake would have preferred steel be added and welded to the angle irons, but the posts would have to do. They'd provide some minimal amount of deflection and at least start the blast moving more in one direction. The fact that the trucks would be parked beside the buildings, and between the buildings and one or more rows of trucks, would provide some additional assist.

Along with the men were three women. They learned that two of the women would be helping assemble the explosives. The third, an elderly and somewhat frail-looking woman was there to prepare food and ensure the others had plenty of tea and water. The men walked into the barn to look over the supplies delivered so far.

In the barn, there were pallets of paper barrels covered with plastic to help keep them dry in case of any rain that might occur. Da had prepared a contingency for most anything that could impact the explosives and their components. The paper barrels were designed for dry food and chemical storage. They were about one meter tall and 1/2 meter in diameter holding a little over 200 liters of volume. Next to the paper barrels were plastic barrels. These looked to Jake to be about 15 gallons in size. They were liquid containers with a 60-liter capacity. These barrels were plastic with a gasket lid - so far, so good. Off to one side, there was a pallet stacked with a bunch of smaller barrels

Jake asked Da, "What's in the small paper barrels?"

Da, "Magnesium powder from firework factory."

Jake, "Then what's in the little red sack next to that, more magnesium?"

Da, "No, thermite from mines to the west."

Jake smiled at that and then said, "Bang on! Let's see the detonators and stuff."

Da ushered them to a table with several boxes on it and several larger boxes on the floor next to it. He opened some of the boxes and tipped one for Jake to see. It was loaded with circuit boards and other electronics. The stuff they needed for the remote triggers. Another of the boxes had blasting caps in it. Jake opened a box on the floor that was filled with wire. He immediately started shaking his head. Da reacted with, "What wrong?"

Jake, "My list called for specific colors of wire. Nowhere in that list did I ask for pink wire. I asked for red wire - red like a fire truck red – not pink." He then opened another box that had blue, black, and green wire. No reaction. Then he opened a third and started shaking his head again. "Again…again with the wrong color! I did not ask for yellow wire. I asked for white wire. Where are the white wire and the red wire?" Followed by a bit of Irish slang, "This is a haymes!"

Da, "That is the white wire and that is the red wire." He was pointing at the wire Jake called out as yellow and the red wire he said was pink.

Jake pulled a length of the 'white' wire off the spool in the box. He then lifted his shirt revealing the t-shirt beneath and pulled that out a bit. Finally, he held the 'white' wire against the shirt to show that it was not the same 'white' as the t-shirt and said. "This," holding the t-shirt and shaking it, "is WHITE!" Then he shook the wire and said, "THIS is YELLOW!" Jake then threw the end of the wire back into the box and stomped out of the barn yelling, "This is total shite!"

Da rolled his eyes. He was told by Art that one of Jake's 'issues', related to his condition, was a crazy obsession with details. Some things we might consider as important were not important to Jake while other, mundane, things were overly important. Da called out to Jake, "I fix the wire for you. I fix it quick." He thought about texting Art, but he knew Art would say, *I told you so*. Instead, Da called the guy he knew to get the proper color wire. That conversation did not go well, but a promise was made to have the correct wire early the next day.

While they waited for the wire and remaining material to arrive, Jimbo helped with the retrofit work on the trucks. Jake just sat and stared out at the open field in front of the barn and the mountains in the distance.

On day two, early in the morning, the wire arrived. With Jake's approval of the colors, he went to work on the triggers. He measured the truck beds and began cutting the wire to length. He cut, stripped, soldered, and taped like a well-oiled machine. He was, after all, a man with a mission.

Simultaneously, Jimbo started work on loading the barrels with what they had. He instructed the helpers to load a layer of thermite into the bottom of a barrel, then a layer of cardboard, and then a layer of magnesium followed with another layer of cardboard. He had Da instruct the workers to be careful and in the process he picked up the Chinese word for it, which he repeated like a broken record.

As Jake completed a detonator assembly he'd stack it neatly on an empty pallet. Late in the day, the diesel fuel arrived, but still no ammonium nitrate.

Day three was like day two as they had to wait for the ammonium nitrate before assembly could be completed. Barrels were loaded as much as they could be and set aside for completion. Jake wrapped up the detonator assembly and started on the triggers. By the end of day three, the first pallets of ammonium nitrate rolled in. It was too late and too dark to start in on the final build of the explosives so the team called it a day, and went to bed. The next morning would be the start of some harder work.

Days four and five were where the heavy lifting took place, literally. Jimbo and his little team would start with a small plastic barrel and a detonator. Jimbo would lower the detonator into the smaller barrel and hold it in place. Once the detonator was positioned into the center of the barrel the two women would pour a quantity of ammonium nitrate around it. Once they had the calculated amount of ammonium nitrate in the barrel they filled it with diesel fuel. Next, they punched a hole in the plastic barrel lid for the wires to pass through, threaded the wires through the hole, and sealed the barrel and around the wires. The two men then raised the completed plastic barrel above the lip of the paper barrel and lowered it carefully. Next a mix of magnesium powder and thermite was added between the inner and outer barrels, sufficient to surround and cover the inner barrel. Finally, the lid to the paper barrel was similarly punched for the wires and clamped and secured to the barrel.

Barrels were loaded and prepped and then stacked four to a pallet and wrapped with cello to hold them tightly together. Once completed a pallet was loaded into the truck, strapped into place and Jake then completed the wiring to that set. They loaded eight pallets on the truck bed and eight more on top of those. Everything was wired to a battery-powered remote trigger that Jake had built and tested along with a failsafe backup, just in case. Once a truck was completed two more sets of stacked pallets were added at the back so that any inspection would reveal crates of packaging materials in sufficient quantities to not prompt suspicion as to the true nature of the remaining contents. By carefully filling and sealing the inner plastic containers – no hint of diesel fuel could be smelled. Each completed truck would provide an explosive force equivalent to six tons of TNT.

During this fury of activity, team Dragons Breath exchanged messages, via Da, with team Hell-Fire to keep tabs on progress and discuss strategy and construction. Although the details for each team's construction were slightly different, they had the same basic plan, components, and combination of chemicals. They did ensure that the triggers for the many truck bombs would be activated from an identical set of remotes, just in case the remotes got mixed up. Both teams were completed one day early, which was great news for Art.

Once Jake had completed the triggers and remotes he moved on to building the shaped charges for the fuel depot retaining wall. For that, he enlisted one of Da's mechanics to cut some metal plates and fashion the tabs that would be used to secure it to the concrete wall. The mechanic also fashioned a few short braces that would swing out and had a hole for a ground anchor to attach.

Next he was on to the bomb that Soo Lin would use, which was fitted into a backpack with a short pull cord and a safety. Removing the safety and then pulling the cord would arm the device giving a five-second delay – just in case. It would give Soo a tiny bit, or as Jake would say, "a wee bit'", of safety margin when the package was dropped, so as not to blow her out of the sky. Lastly, he built out a simple incendiary device and remote. The device could attach to the frame or any metal part of the lab van and had provisions for other means of securing it, just in case. It would ignite a bit of the ammonium nitrate and diesel fuel from within a small flask and then – a fiery boom.

Da was tasked to get the devices and their triggers to the proper individuals and in time to ensure they could be ready for the big night.

* * *

Freedom bar factory

At the 'Freedom' bar factory, Duyi watched and waited for a truck filled with bad rice to leave the plant. It was three days before a container truck was fully loaded and left the facility. He followed it with ease as it made its way to the port in Shanghai. There it was loaded onto the container ship named "Golden Star" of the Shuang export company. He milled around the dock and eventually learned the ship was leaving port the next day. Duyi contacted Da and relayed the info. Da sent that on to Art who had it transmitted to Joanna.

When the ship left port, it was immediately tracked and followed, at a safe, distance by a U.S. submarine. They would follow it to the port of Los Angeles where U.S. Customs agents would seize the ship and its contents for inspection. CDC personnel located the container and moved it to a secure location. The contents and the container would be destroyed. The crew would be held without the ability to make a call to China until the mission was complete.

* * *

Yiyang

Jiaguo headed to Yiyang, where he would provide the cover for Soo Lin's crop dusting operation. Once there he met up with one of Da's contacts and received the gear he'd need for the assignment. Included were the protective coveralls and mask along with a Chinese QBZ-191 sniper rifle from the early part of the 21st century. It was equipped with a 1-5x power night vision scope, which was more than sufficient for Jiaguo's needs. He also received a pair of older model American made night vision goggles.

After looking over the equipment and making sure it was clean and functioning well, he spent time milling around with the locals and occasionally hiking around the rice facility. Later in the week, he made a few nighttime recon trips with the goggles, including climbing a few trees from which to choose a vantage point. He settled on one tree that allowed him to get high up, see the grounds, and cover everything but the narrow far end of the building. He expected that might be the only safe place for the guards when the shooting started, but he'd have to leave it as he could not cover it from a single elevated position. Now all he had left to do was sit tight and wait.

* * *

Soo Lin

Before heading off on her special assignment with Art, Soo Lin secured the crop spraying plane she would be using for the rice farm. She located a farm about halfway between the target city of Yiyang and Yuanjiang to the north where she was able to negotiate storage for her plane. She explained to the old farmer that she had some work coming in the area and needed a place to park the plane that was close to the work and not in the city. This farm had enough of a hard flat field that she could land and takeoff. With that, the plane was secured and ready for the chemicals and bomb. She notified Da via Art of the plane's location so the chemicals could be delivered and loaded in her absence.

* * *

The Lab

Hungqu made his way to the stakeout location at the Lab. There he encountered some vagrant kids crashing in the empty apartment and very quietly persuaded them to disappear and not let him see them again. He stashed his rifle and tracer rounds in a closet that had a hole in the interior wall. Once the rifle was in there it was not noticeable, but would be easy to remove when needed. He'd handle that after the van was wired and he was not going to need to be away from the room again.

Feng was given the name of one of Da's contacts that would be handling the fuel tanks at the Lab. Once he made contact he was given a place to stay and an opportunity to meet the other men helping with the mission task. All that remained was to sit and wait.

DR. YĪSHĒNG
TWO DAYS BEFORE DRAGON DOWN

Dai had taken a commercial plane up to Beijing and proceeded to a warehouse on the airport property. There he encountered an older woman who confirmed that she was appointed by Da. She handed Dai a duffle and a small tool bag. She then left without speaking. In the duffle, Dai found maintenance worker clothes and an id badge, which he promptly put on. He took the tool bag and left the warehouse in an official airport maintenance pickup truck heading for hangar 12.

Once at the hangar, Dai approached the single military guard stationed motionless at the rear of Stephanie's private jet. He was a Shi warrior and could have swiftly and silently dispatched the guard and hidden the body on the plane, but that might have raised an alarm if discovered. Instead, he approached the guard and began to explain his assigned maintenance tasks. The guard reviewed the documents, searched the tool bag, and after verifying all was well, waved Dai on to complete his task. Dai boarded the plane.

In the cockpit, Dai removed a small device from his tool bag and proceeded to dismantle the transponder. He located the wire harness, described perfectly in Soo Lin's instructions, and attached the device to it. The device's wires were routed under the instrument panel and attached to a loose connector used for instrument testing. He then returned the transponder to its original position, intact and functional.

Having completed his task, Dai left the plane and bowed to the guard before exiting the hangar. Others would be arriving soon to complete the next part of the mission.

* * *

Dongguan Lab

MSA070771LMC, "Doctor Yīshēng, MSA receives encrypted message from Chairman Zháng Wei Jun – Urgent."

Dr. Yīshēng quickly looks around the room to ensure they are alone then says, "Proceed LMC."

MSA-LMC, "Urgent – inform Doctor Yīshēng and MSA to proceed to hangar 12 Beijing airport – private jet Wolff number 29N37G tomorrow, 5 PM . Destination Hong Kong, reason secret. Private jet waiting at Dongguan airport private hangar #147A to transport Y and MSA to Beijing. Zero communication – passport will be provided in Hong Kong. Acknowledge receipt of message immediately."

Dr. Yīshēng looked at his watch, "Acknowledge message – affirmative, LMC. Make sure you have downloaded all current information about the work we have done here. Call for transport to Dongguan airport before you upload the data, bring this laptop."

Dr. Yīshēng didn't need to repeat his instructions, MSA-LMC was reliable. He considered going to his home first but he knew that if the Chairman had sent an encrypted message that there was an urgent reason and detailing no contact with anyone, he best not. He could not even consider asking for more information when the Chairman issued such a directive.

When the Doctor exited the building he was surprised to see that the MSA-LMC was waiting in the car in advance of his arrival at the curb. This MSA had received other instructions from its administrator, Goose. This MSA had already been programmed with flight plans for the trip, courtesy of Dave Tillis, one of Savior Unit's white hat hackers in the U.S. The program was a type of self-decommission program. At exactly 6:45 PM, this MSA would decommission itself and become the equivalent of a can of smelt.

This droid's outward appearance was identical to the MSA-LMC, but it had no history other than its most basic language skills, recognition of the face of Dr. Yīshēng, and advanced flight instruction for small jets. The order to take his laptop with it when the car arrived to drive them to the airport's private hangar was the droid's primary command. Second, to that, it would deliver the programmed flight plan to the airport tower in addition to the actual auto-pilot flight path to download into the jet's computer. Dr. Yīshēng's flight from Donnguan left promptly at 2:30 PM.

Goose wondered if the decommissioning of this droid would elicit a feeling of remorse, as Joshua had demonstrated when they had had to dispose of his car back in Texas. Goose had no extensive relationship with this droid, so the question was irrelevant.

***

Beijing – Stephanie's jet

Shortly before Doctor Yīshēng arrived at the Beijing airport, Stephanie Wolff's pilot had received a text message stating that she urgently needed to meet him to discuss a trip, and the details, at her hotel. He was to meet her at the hotel's bar before dinner. It was an offer he could not refuse.

At 4:30 PM CCT Doctor Yīshēng's flight from Dongguan touched down at Beijing airport. After disembarking he was met by the pilot of Stephanie's plane. She introduced herself as Soo and proceeded to inform the doctor of their flight plan. They would be flying over the China Sea and around the east shore of Taiwan on their approach to Hong Kong. She told him the plane was ready and they would be leaving in a few minutes, once her final inspection was completed.

At 4:45 PM they boarded Stephanie's plane and the MSA took a seat in the faraday compartment behind the cockpit. This compartment protected the plane's sensitive instrumentation and communications equipment, during takeoffs and landings, from any possible interference of the MSA's sophisticated electronics. The MSA had no 'airplane mode', but would be free to move about the cabin once they were airborne.

The pilot assisted the Doctor to his seat, handed him the laptop the MSA had been carrying and went through the normal safety instructions. She asked that the Doctor set his private phone to Airplane mode, which he did without hesitation. As she moved to the cockpit she pulled the curtain separating the passenger compartment from the front of the plane.

The pilot released the MSA from the faraday compartment and it quietly moved to the pilot seat. The pilot removed her cap, pink wig, and jacket placing them on the MSA, and then quickly pulled on a pair of maintenance coveralls and a headset. She stepped off the plane and secured the door. Soo then moved the plane from inside the hangar to the apron and decoupled and parked the tug. Completing her 'ground crew' tasks she walked by the guard, who failed to question how it was that she was in the area, and exited the hangar.

The droid did as instructed, and uploaded the flight plan. It then proceeded to taxi the plane from the hangar and onto the taxiway. Meanwhile, Soo was walking to her private jet and using the headset to communicate with the tower performing the normal two-way chat to obtain permission to leave. Once cleared, the droid moved to the designated runway and Stephanie's jet left for Hong Kong. Departure time: 5:04 PM.

The guard would remain steadfast at his post until relieved. It would be several hours before he would be questioned by his superiors about the plane's departure.

* * *

Beijing – Soo's Jet

Dai, Soo, Art, Goose, and MSA-LMC boarded Soo's private jet shortly after Doctor Yīshēng's plane had left the ground. Once Soo was certain all was ok to disconnect from the tower communications she pulled off her radio headset and announced, "Doctor is in the air. We are clear to go."

Art, "So Dai, any problems?"

Dai, "Very smooth Art, no problems."

Soo performed an inspection of the plane and prepped for take-off. It would be 30 more minutes before they would be able to get off the ground in Beijing due to heavy air traffic. By then the Doctor would be halfway to Taiwan and somewhere over the East China Sea.

* * *

Stephanie's Jet

As soon as the plane was in the air, Dr. Yīshēng opened the laptop and turned it on. It booted into the typical welcome screen of a newly installed operating system. *This is odd*, thought the Doctor. He proceeded through a few prompts and finally obtained access to the familiar desktop, but without his familiar applications. He navigated the laptop's contents and found none of the records he had instructed LMC to load before leaving the Lab. This would not do.

He got up from his seat before the fasten seatbelt sign was off and threw back the curtain to question LMC only to find that LMC was not where it was supposed to be. He then retrieved his phone and attempted communication with the droid, but the phone was in Airplane mode. He turned off Airplane mode only to find that the phone would not return to normal communication and was locked in Airplane mode. He rebooted the phone and tried again, with the same unsuccessful result, finally throwing it against the cabin wall.

He then proceeded to pound on the locked cockpit door and call out for the pilot to open the door and explain what had happened to his LMC. There was no response. The plane continued to climb to its assigned altitude of 4500 meters (just under 15,000 feet).

Frantic now, the Doctor rushed to the back of the plane to find the secured virus containers and was pleased to see they were all there as expected. Four refrigerated containers were strapped securely to the compartment with metal bindings and strong locked latches. Next, he tapped the control panel on one to check the temperature and to his horror, the display read 8.0°C! Out loud he exclaimed, "No! No! No!" He checked another and then another until all four showed temperatures near 8.0°C. All should have read -5.0°C. He knew that at temperatures exceeding 20.0°C the virus would be destroyed. He turned and stormed to the cockpit - the pilot must return to Beijing or Dongguan whichever was closest to their current location! His precious cargo was dying and it needed to be saved!

Meanwhile, the plane had entered into the airspace of the Taiwan air traffic control center and out of range of the Shanghai Controllers. It was making good time using the trade winds to get a speed boost. The droid had placed the plane on auto-pilot and was sitting motionless with eyes forward despite the incessant pounding, of all manner of things, on the cockpit door as the Doctor attempted to break in or break it down.

After quite some time the Doctor had finally given up and was sitting on the floor, nearly catatonic, when he heard the latch on the door unlock. He mustered the strength to get up and open the door. He immediately screamed in hoarse tones a series of questions in mixed Chinese and English. "What have you done to MY virus? Where are we? Why is my phone not working? Where is my LMC? " On and on he went in his tirade.

The motionless droid then began to move and touch various controls on the instrument panel and above its head. It took the plane off auto-pilot and proceeded to increase speed and altitude. A few minutes later a barely audible pop was heard as the transponder was disconnected from all power and turned off. The device that Dai installed was set to trigger above an altitude of 4572 meters (exactly, 15,000 feet).

* * *

Utah, U.S.A.

At the NSA in Bluffdale, Utah, Dave Tillis' team was monitoring the flight and radar in Taiwan, the Philippines, and China. The plane was crossing air traffic control boundaries where its ownership would switch between entities. The transponder was the normal thing to disappear first and then the blip on a controller's screen as a plane switched from one air traffic control station to another. As it should, the plane disappeared on the Taiwan air traffic controller's screen, but never was picked up on another controller station.

After, there would be some communication between entities for the handoff and then on the odd behavior, but the plane was gone and flight records in the databases showed no such plane was ever tracked.

* * *

Back on Stephanie's jet

The plane had continued climbing and quickly reached an altitude of 6000 meters (~20,000 feet) and leveled off. It was nowhere near the filed flight plan but was quickly nearing its destination. The Doctor was about to attack the pilot when he finally realized it was his dedicated LMC in a pink wig. The next thing he did, or more aptly put, screamed was, "What have you done with my data? Where is my data? You must format the laptop and download the formulae immediately!" The droid did not speak or turn its head; it simply sat facing forward with its hands on the controls, its eyes blinking and blinking. It had no program stating that this human was the administrator and had no understanding of the commands being shouted at it. There were no formulae stored in MSA's warehouse.

The Doctor took hold of the droids right hand on the throttle and turned it to see the designator ID on its wrist – "MSA_u1Nsht". Not his personal LMC, but some other MSA. For just a split second the Doctor focused on the MSA's ID. *u1Nsht? What is u 1N sht?* Then he realized he was doomed - his body went numb. The droid returned its hand to the throttle control, turned to the Doctor, and said, "How may I please you Doctor Yīshēng?" It pushed the yoke and throttle forward – the plane started a downward dive. The time was: 6:45 PM.

* * *

Soo's plane

Soo Lin put her jet on auto-pilot. Dai was sitting quietly in the co-pilot's seat enjoying the view out the windshield and the colorful instrument panel. As she left the cockpit she said to Dai, with an unquestionable sense of confidence, "You touch anything and I kill you, Shi warrior." Dai found that funny at first and smiled, but quickly turned that off as she left for the passenger compartment. *Maybe*, he thought. *Maybe she could.*

In the passenger compartment, she sat down next to Art who was holding a tablet with some video on it. "What that?" she asked.

Art said with a smile, "This is the view of Stephanie's plane through the eyes of the pilot. You just missed the Doctor finally getting into the cockpit. He's a little confused and very pissed off."

Soo, "He got long to go?"

Art, "Nope. Watch."

Soo leaned over and wrapped her arm around Art's arm and put her free hand on it, gently squeezing his bicep. On the video, she only saw the view out the cockpit windshield and some of the instrument panel. She leaned in to see the altimeter and noted the 6000-meter attitude immediately. "Ooh, he's going to go down now!" She knew what had been programmed into the MSA, now in command of the plane, and it was about to put the plane in a nosedive from almost 20,000 feet.

Art, "Yup. Here we go." Other than looking at the instruments it was hard to tell the plane was diving. Of course, the Doctor was screaming again and alarms started going off. The droid turned its head again to view the Doctor. The g-forces of the dive had him pinned to the bulkhead of the cockpit where he would remain for the next 20 seconds or so. The droid then looked forward again.

Soo and Art could start to make out little white and gold sparkles through the plane's windshield as the setting sun highlighted the waves of the approaching sea. After that it got harder to see much of anything in the video with the plane shaking violently now. A few seconds later the feed stopped.

* * *

Somewhere in the South China Sea

The plane disappeared some 400 kilometers due east of Hong Kong and well south of Taiwan. The wreckage would never be found. The speed of the plane at impact was over 600 miles per hour. The fuselage was crumpled, nearly half its length, crushing the Doctor instantly upon impact. The virus containers had reached an internal temperature over 25°C – the virus was cooked. The wings would be torn off at impact and sink shortly thereafter, but the rest of the plane would make its final approach on the ocean floor and come to rest some 2200 meters below.

* * *

Changsha Airport

Soo Lin, Art, Wei, and the two droids flew into the Changsha Huanghua International Airport in Changsha. The airport was about an hour's drive from Yiyang where the rice farm was located and about an hour and a half from where Soo had stashed the plane. They were going to part ways for now with Art having some unfinished business in Beijing. He would be arranging for a car and be staying overnight. He expected to be in Beijing on Dragon Down day.

After getting off the plane Soo turned to Art and threw her arms around him. She turned her head and placed it firmly against his chest, then said, "I want you to stay."

Art put his arms around her shoulders and pulled her close and told her, "I really would like to, but I have business I have to get to in Beijing and you have a vital assignment to complete."

Soo, "I know, but I want you to stay."

Art, "I know. We can be together again, just be safe and come to me in Hawaii."

Soo, "I will be safe. Will you promise we can be together?"

Art, "On my honor, I promise."

Soo released her hold on Art and wiped a tear from her

cheek, "You be careful too."

Art, "You bet."

Goose then said, "`Miss Soo, Goose will be happy to see you on beach.`"

Soo, "I bet you would." After which she walked off to head to Yiyang for her wild crop spraying ride.

Goose gave one blink.

DRAGON DOWN

Dongguan

At 1:48 AM China Central Time on a Tuesday in early summer, an unmarked truck drove down Zanshu road on the west side of the petroleum storage facility. It swerved gently to the left onto the shoulder and promptly ran over the power and communication distribution box that fed and transmitted surveillance video to a state security station 3.5 kilometers away. The truck made its way back onto the road and turned right at the next street leaving a trail of oil from its ruptured oil pan. Two streets over a hooded figure in dark clothes left the truck at the side of the road and disappeared into the night.

As promised, Art had reached out to the Savior Unit's Dave Tillis at the NSA. He asked that China's communication infrastructure experience an 'anomaly' for several minutes just before and after 2:00 AM CCT. Dave, who would become known by the very respectful moniker of 'Miracle Man' had his guys create a massive, simultaneous, systems update and reboot of the Chinese internet, phones, and communication infrastructure devices and satellites. And, make it appear to have originated from a small abandoned house near Hangzhou, not far from Shanghai.

At 1:50 AM, exactly, a second smaller truck entered the area just below the railroad offload station and turned to take a position for the tank farm part of the op. The driver spotted a figure standing over the demolished communication box and said in Chinese, "Company."

Feng, softly responded, "Continue to op, I will take the intruder." He then slipped out the back door and stepped off the truck. He made his way to a large utility pole for cover. The truck continued past the intruder, rounded the southwest corner of the tank farm, and pulled up to the southeast corner of the storage tank spill retaining wall.

With the intruder distracted Feng approached from behind and found a small figure in black pants wearing a not-so-clean pink hoodie. He stopped an arms-length behind it and said, "Hello." The intruder let out a high pitched squeak while turning to see who was behind them. Feng saw a young woman's face and, while having extensive martial arts and weapons training, determined that only minimal force was needed to subdue her. Two quick open hand moves and the young woman crumpled to the ground. Feng quickly bound her hands and carried her to the truck where he would further restrain her before taking an overlook position for the tank farm crew.

While Feng was engaged with the intruder, the three remaining men exited the truck. They quickly moved ladders, tools, and the suitcases containing shaped charges over the three-meter high concrete wall. Two men made their way to the storage tank supply outlet piping, while another positioned himself at the retaining wall. When Feng finished with the young woman he took a position to stand guard and monitored the area.

At the same time, a truck with three men pulled up to large railroad tank cars at the fuel load/unload area 75 meters away and slightly uphill from the storage tank facility. The men at the railroad transfer facility moved quickly to attach three 20 meter sets of 10cm connection hoses to the three fully loaded fuel tank cars nearest them. They promptly opened the outlet valves allowing diesel fuel to pour out and down the slight incline toward the storage tanks below. The fuel spill made its way around the west side of the fuel containment retaining wall and then toward the lab and smoke bomb facility parking area. Elapsed time was 3 minutes and 30 seconds.

One of the three men at the fuel tanks removed from the suitcases, and placed, two shaped charge satchels along the base of the retaining wall. He proceeded to attach them using a concrete nail gun covered with several blankets to subdue the noise and flash from the cartridges as they fired the nails into the wall. The other two men were using battery-powered impact guns to remove the 40 bolts securing a 90 degree fitting on the 25cm outlet supply line from one of the tanks at the facility. The shaped charges were in place, with a lightweight blast blanket protecting them, in four minutes. One minute later a thump could be heard as the wall opened up. It would be two more minutes before the fuel supply outlet fitting was removed and the tank outlet valve opened creating a small river of diesel fuel flowing downhill toward the Lab – exactly as planned. Elapsed time was 7 minutes and 42 seconds.

At the security building, the ranking officer dispatched two subordinate officers to investigate the loss of video from the fuel storage facility. By 1:52 AM the two officers were on their way. It would take approximately seven more minutes for them to arrive at the facility. By this time Feng and Da's men, at the fuel storage facility, had scrambled over the wall and were on the road heading away from the facility while the stream of fuel poured from the outlet supply pipe joined by the fuel pouring over the road from the tank cars above.

As the security vehicle approached the facility the

officers noticed liquid running across the road apparently from the railroad tracks, which was odd given that the night was clear and dry. They stopped to investigate and heard but did not see the truck below them turning a corner and speeding away with its lights turned off. They encountered the strong smell of diesel fuel. One officer used his radio, which was not affected by the temporary communication blackout, to frantically inform the security station's ranking officer of the fuel spill and river of fluid running across the road. Not one of the officers knew about the work being performed at the facility down the hill where fuel was now collecting around the Lab building.

About one kilometer away Hungqu observed the Lab area with a powerful night vision rifle scope. Once he was satisfied that the lab was sufficiently flooded with fuel he pressed a button on his remote detonator and the incendiary charge under the hood of the Lab's delivery truck ignited, setting the entire area around the lab on fire. The blaze turned the night sky orange and began to creep up the hill toward the storage tanks. He was pleased to see the flames rising around the building. Hungqu smiled and softly said to himself, "Not bad."

The security officers heard the bang of the small explosion to their left and turned to see the fire beginning to grow and move in their direction. They jumped back in their vehicle and the driver gunned the engine. The vehicle stood still for a moment - it was still in 'Park'. The officer in the passenger seat yelled "走" ("GO!") at the driver, who then slammed the transmission shifter into reverse without taking his foot off the pedal. The vehicle lurched and sped backward. The passenger again yelled "走, 走, 走 !" ("GO, GO, GO!")

Seconds later the fire reached the first tank and an orange flash was observed by the officers frantically leaving the scene. Immediately after, another small explosion was heard and the tank ruptured at the base spilling a now raging river of fire toward the already engulfed lab. Seconds after that, the fuel vapors ignited in the nearly empty tank and it exploded sending a huge ball of fire skyward and pieces of tank structure flying in all directions. Some of the pieces pierced the other tanks and more explosions rocked the area. Hungqu spoke once more to himself, "Not bad at all." Time: 2:02 AM. He stashed the weapon and gear in the closet wall and left the building on foot.

Three kilometers from the Lab, Feng had Da's driver pull over. He removed the young woman from the back of the truck and released her bonds. She would have some neck pain for a few days but was otherwise unharmed. He stood behind her and softly spoke into her ear while having her face away from the truck. "I was in control of your fate a few moments ago and bestowed mercy upon you. Go now my gazelle and run like the wind. Do not look back, do not stop." With that, the woman bolted and, indeed, ran like a gazelle.

It would be two days and over 40 injured firefighters before the fire was finally out. All that remained of the Lab campus was structural steel - bent and mangled from the intense heat. Everything else was rendered to piles of ash and melted metal. The Lab and the virus were no more...

* * *

Tianjin – Bottling Plant

Jake could not resist watching the fireworks and chose to grab an executive hotel suite on the 42nd floor of the Beijing Princess Hotel, 3.5 kilometers northwest of the Tianjin docks. It was a perfect view to the east and a very comfortable room with a balcony. He was joined by his partner in crime, Jimbo, whom he had to convince to join him for the spectacle. Jimbo was somewhat concerned about being in the area, but Jake's freedom from fear made it too easy to convince Jimbo to join him.

Hours earlier, at just before 10:00 PM CCT, the six

trucks and drivers arrived at the bottling plant. There was a bit of confrontation at the facility's main gate when the lead driver was challenged by Security as plant workers poured through the exit. He argued that his men needed to get home and that he had no patience for other people's screw-ups. He provided paperwork and invoices for the trucks and after a quick inspection, they were permitted to enter.

The trucks stopped at previously identified points along the two sides of the long building. Each driver carefully positioned his load next to, but inside the rows of trucks already parked there – three trailers along each long wall of the building. They would set the trailers in place, uncouple, and leave the premises with a wave to the guards for allowing them to complete their work and return to their families. Now it was only a matter of time.

As zero hour approached, Jake positioned a spotting scope and small rectangular radio transceiver on the hotel balcony. He attached the radio to a power brick and a laptop on which he had loaded and calibrated his custom remote trigger app. The app would connect briefly to the devices in the trucks and confirm activity. Once that was done he ordered room service for himself and Jimbo.

At 10 minutes to 2:00 AM, the laptop chirped a reminder. Both men put their earplugs in and sat back in comfortable lounge chairs. One of the drivers was still on the road and safely away from the plant. He dialed the plant security desk number from a disposable phone and reported a bomb was on the premises.

The security guard was incredulous at first, but the driver insisted and further reinforced the story by telling the guard it was he who had planted it. The guard recorded the call in his log. The truck driver tossed the phone and continued home. The building was not evacuated.

On the far side of the building, one of the security guards stepped out a door to have a smoke. He fished out a cigarette from his pack and proceeded to light it. One flick of the lighter and no flame. "拉屎"(shit) he said out loud. Flick, flick, flick – still no flame. He was getting angry now. More flicks and nothing, but then, on lucky number eight, he got a flame and ... It was exactly 2:00 AM, Jake had put on a pair of sunglasses and tapped the 'Enter' key on his laptop.

There was no delay between the trigger and any of the trailers receiving the signal. All six detonated at once. The blasts went off in a bright flash thanks to the magnesium powder and thermite. The light was so bright that those who saw it first thought it was a nuclear explosion. The powerful blast blew in the exterior walls of the building and sent a column of orange and black fire and smoke over 500 meters into the night sky. The resulting cloud formed the classic mushroom shape and reinforced fears of a nuclear bomb.

The shock wave reached the hotel some 10 seconds later and shook the building. "Savage", Jake said softly. Buildings in close proximity to the plant were not so lucky. Within one-kilometer buildings suffered damage and most windows were broken with interior damage due to falling objects and furniture. Some had roofs collapse. Those less than 1/2 kilometer from the blast sustained fire damage or were destroyed entirely. The blast registered 2.9 on the Richter scale.

Buildings further out suffered minor structural damage and less glass breakage. The abandoned silos near the plant, that were slated for demolition, were toppled – portions of them fell into the river channel. The worker housing on the far side of the river channel also sustained damage, but none so great as to cause serious injuries or fires.

After the initial blast, the entire plant was engulfed in sustained flames that towered over 100 meters into the night sky. Ambulances, security, police, firefighters, and others would arrive within minutes of the blasts using emergency ground radio communications. Some firefighters would suffer burns when they first attempted to put down the massive flames by spraying water on the magnesium and thermite still burning after the initial blast. Eventually, the authorities would determine that several means of containing the fire would be the best they could do – they'd let the place burn itself out while protecting surrounding buildings.

The security guards and maintenance workers in the plant at the time would become names and pictures of those lost, in newspaper articles. Only the body of the security guard at the front of the building near the main entrance would be recovered – what was left of it. The others would become lost in the mountain of ash left behind.

Jake and Jimbo gathered their things and left the hotel that night to ensure they would be far away before an investigation was launched. They took a plane to the Yunnan province before any air travel could be canceled and then made their way to Laos as planned.

* * *

Shanghai Freedom Bar Facility

The men delivering the trucks to the 'Freedom' bar facility did not encounter the same security scrutiny as the men at the bottling plant. Here the trucks were waved through with a smile from the guard. The drivers had their assignments and proceeded to park the trailers as planned.

Two trailers were parked by the target building C with one on either side, right up next to the building. They were placed so closely that a normal man could not slip between the building and the trailer – even shimmying sideways. The other trailers were similarly parked, two on opposite sides of building A and two on opposite sides of building B. All of the drivers left without incident and were well on their way before the dragon's fury would be unleashed.

Both Wham and Lightnin' were setting up for the trigger

event. They had pulled together their gear and hiked up a hill to the south of the facility about 2.8 kilometers away. They figured they would look like a couple of amateur astronomers, just in case, but weren't expecting to be stopped by anyone. The hill was far enough away to be safe, and with a line of sight view of the buildings. Like Jake and Jimbo, they set up the spotting scope, radio, and laptop at approximately 1:30 AM CCT. Well before 2:00 AM they had things tested and ready to go.

At about 1:45 AM there was a rustling in the brush near where they were setup. Despite their military experience, and not having had the curse of a birth defect like the fearless Jake, they nearly crapped their pants. Turned out it was a small, hungry, cat. Wham scooped it up and Lightnin' double-checked the gear.

At 1:58 AM Lightnin' made a call to the facility's security number to report a bomb on the property. These guards pulled a fire alarm, called it into their main office, and exited the building.

At 2:00 AM, Lightnin' looked at Wham and asked, "Ready?"

Wham wrapped the small cat into his coat pulling it to his chest and replied, "Ready." With that Lightnin' tapped the 'Enter' key on the laptop.

The simultaneous explosions lit up the night sky with a bright white flash followed by telltale orange and black fire and smoke shooting straight up followed by the mushroom cloud formation. The security guards were just over 40 meters away and behind a slight hump in the road when the blast went off and were thrown to the ground by the shockwave. Bits of fiery material landed around them. They would be injured and in shock but would survive.

The same could not be said for the three buildings. They all experienced their brick and metal walls being pushed inward and collapsing. Almost as if the buildings had imploded on themselves. The minor reinforcement the workers had performed on all the trailers was just enough to help send a good portion of the blast laterally into the buildings.

The proximity of the building C trailers was a bonus as that caused the roof of the building to be blown more than 60 meters into the air before being ripped apart and sending shards of steel and aluminum flying over 200 meters in all directions. In an instant, the building was no more. All that would remain was the burned-out carcasses of some heavy equipment and the mangled structural steel of the building's skeleton.

Wham and Lightnin' were knocked back but recovered to watch the action of the first responders. Later they would retreat to Lightnin's relatives to spend the rest of the night and then head back to the site in the morning to survey their handy work – Wham's new pet cat in tow.

The lead commander of the firefighters was smart enough not to start applying water immediately. He had one crew spray water away from the fire and move their stream toward the fire slowly. As soon as the water mixed with the burning magnesium and thermite the water itself burst into flames. The magnesium/thermite fire was so hot that the water molecules would split. Oxygen would combine with the magnesium to form combustible chemicals and hydrogen gas. He called for non-water based fire chemicals and foam to fight the fire.

In the end, there were many injuries, but no fatalities at the facility or in the surrounding area. Other buildings would suffer extensive damage and some would burn and be no more, but there was no human collateral damage and the mission was a decisive success.

* * *

Yiyang Rice Farm
Soo reached the farm before dark and prepped the plane for flight. It was a Hongdu N-5 single-engine plane with

low wings that could handle fuel, cargo, and pilot with a total weight of 1000 kilos. Soo needed to move the plane from the barn to the field for take-off. When she tried to move the loaded plane she found herself slipping on the earthen floor. *Great*, she thought, *how am I gonna move this?*

She could have started the plane in the barn and taxied it out, but that would have gotten a lot of dried grass, dirt, and other junk flying around – she couldn't risk it. Of course, she was on a farm and that farmer had a small, very old, tractor. It took her a few tries to start the thing, but she got the tractor running and used it to tow the plane out of the barn. Once in the air, she'd be about 10 minutes from the target.

So at 1:45 AM CCT she climbed in with the backpack device Jake had made and a pair of night-vision goggles and fired up the plane. She taxied to the far end of the field and tested the sprayers - everything was a go. She pulled the goggles over her head and turned them on. Next, she pushed in on the throttle and started the plane down the field. The ride was bumpy and getting worse as she upped the speed to get off the ground. Soon though, the plane separated from the earth and the ride was smooth again. All she needed to do was get the fully loaded plane over the trees at the end of the field.

A little more throttle and then a little more stick and…still trees in front of her tiny plane. More throttle, more stick, and the plane began to climb. She made a slight bank to the right as the trees were lower in one spot and just skimmed the tops of them with the plane's big tires. She was off – now all she needed was Jiaguo to be in place and all would be fine.

At 1:58 AM she made her first pass over the rice farm. The night vision goggles were a blessing in that she did not need to turn on the landing lights to see the field. She flew in low over the trees, dropped down quickly, and turned on a blast of chemicals. She concentrated on keeping the plane level across the field and shutting off the sprayers while pulling up in time to clear the trees. Each pass would get easier as the plane would get lighter.

After her second pass, the ground lit up from muzzle flashes as the four guards were now attempting to shoot down the intruder with their AK style rifles. Initially, the bullets missed her plane, but eventually one clipped the canopy – a lucky shot. *Where is that sniper?*

In the tree, Jiaguo picked a target on the ground, and with a single shot, that threat was gone. The three remaining guards did not realize there was another intruder with a more lethal offense. A moment later a second guard went down and Soo made another pass. Now the guards had to worry.

That second sniper shot alerted them to the general direction of the fire. They fired wildly in the direction they thought the gunshot came from and missed terribly as they made a hasty retreat to get to the building and use it for cover. The two guards were running, hunched down, with one slightly behind the other still shooting. Soo made another pass. Then another sniper shot. The second guard did not make it. Jiaguo thought, *Three down – one to go*. He was going to need to re-position to get that last one.

By this time Soo had made all the passes she needed in the east/west direction and was switching to a north/south pattern to ensure complete annihilation of the rice. She and her little plane were now in a direct line toward the last guard's position and he took advantage. He opened a volley in full automatic fire mode and the bullets whizzed by Soo's plane. The guard had found the cover he needed behind the building and out of sight of the sniper.

This time Soo was not so lucky and several bullets pierced the aircraft's thin skin. She was unaware of any damage and the plane still flew straight, but she was leaking fuel as a fuel line had been nicked. Unfortunately for the guard, his magazine emptied and he needed to reload at just the moment that Soo dumped a load of the chemical she was carrying on him and the field.

While the chemical was not dangerous to humans unless ingested, he was now soaked. He staggered out from his place of cover wiping his eyes. The guard would not need to worry about medical attention or possible poisoning as he was down and gone with Jiaguo's final shot.

Soo made the last passes and dumped the remaining chemical. She made one final pass with the canopy open and dropped the backpack bomb on the rice farm's building. The explosion rocked the area and almost knocked Jiaguo out of the tree, but he made it safely down. Soo looked back to see she had made a good hit and the building was burning. She banked the plane and headed off - mission accomplished. Jiaguo crawled out of the tree and hiked off to safety.

As Soo approached the farmer's field she noticed her fuel gauge was showing empty and the plane was beginning to sputter. Knowing that she would not be able to return to the landing field she immediately picked out the only road she could see. She lined up the plane with the road and promptly landed on it. The need for haste caused her to land hard and at a higher speed than she would have liked. The large tires bounced on the road and the plane was up again. Down it came again and another bounce. Each bounce would cause the small plane to change direction and forced Soo to wrangle it back with the controls. A few more hard bounces and the plane's speed reduced enough for it to stick to the road and roll to a stop.

She climbed out of the small cockpit and tossed a lighted flare into it to ensure there would be no DNA evidence found. She backed away as the plane began to burn and a moment later the remaining fuel vapor in the wings ignited with a thump. She felt the heat from the flames, then turned and walked the rest of the way to the farm. There she got into her car, and headed to her private jet thinking, *Hawaii, here I come. Or maybe...*

CHAIRMAN ZHÁNG WEI JUN
RECKONING

It is 3:37 AM CCT in Beijing. The Chairman is sitting at his desk in front of staff including ministries of communications, defense, health, commerce, and military. He is known for his commanding voice in normal communications. But his manner tends to inversely and proportionally decrease in volume in response to his increased fury.

Chairman Jun, "What has brought us to this urgent meeting in the middle of my sleep?"

Director of Defense Fu Cheng, "Honorable Chairman, only 45 minutes ago my office was advised of a nine-minute interruption of state communications followed by delayed information declaring that there have been explosions at multiple locations across China..."

Chairman Jun interrupts in a moderated voice demanding, "What do you mean explosions?? Have the laowai committed an act of war against our nation? Have the Americans brought bombs against us? I need someone to get me a line to Vice President Hoge, immediately!"

Director Fu Cheng, "Honorable chairman, from what

we have been able to ascertain, there has been no foreign military action taken, it appears that the bombings may be acts of domestic terrorism."

Chairman Jun in a slightly lower volume continues, "Spare me your speculations, Cheng, lest you and your family spend the remainder of your short lives in re-education! What exactly was bombed and what is the extent of the damage?"

Cheng, "Dongguan Laboratory and smoke bomb facility and Tianjin where the HVD infused water were produced, sir, my reports indicate 100% loss. Shanghai GMO rice and Freedom Bars manufacturing and packaging facility, also 100% loss. The breakdown of communications prevented the notification and deployment of military. Emergency services were able to attempt to mitigate the damages using emergency ground radio communications. The human loss that we've estimated was…"

Chairman Jun, in a still softer voice, stopped Cheng in mid-sentence by signaling his military aide to draw his weapon, "Director Cheng, do you think that I care about the number of the dead, which is about to include your worthless name to the total?"

Cheng understood opting to close his mouth and silently pray for his life which now hangs precariously as the worm on a thread of silk on a windy day.

The Chairman now turns his attention to the Directory of the Ministry of Communications, Li Ying. "Do you bring me news of how communications could be shut down to an entire country and exactly how long this breakdown occurred?"

The director Li Ying, while keeping his eyes fixed on the floor, as reverently as humanly possible, tells the Chairman, "The communication breakdown began at 1:55 AM and ended at 2:04 AM. The worthless dogs who were responsible for monitoring the annunciation systems have been put to death after their questioning revealed no valid reason for their failures, Honorable Chairman. We have teams performing forensics to ascertain the perpetrators involved in the communications breech. The military is also involved in the process of questioning the entire staff of the ministry of communications. The criminals will be identified and questioned to discover others involved before their torture and execution is complete."

Chairman Jun, "Go now and let your face not touch a pillow until you bring me the information you seek."

Director Li Ying departs as quickly and silently as possible, thanking the heavens that he has an opportunity to live another day.

Chairman Jun turns to Minister of Commerce, Chow Lu. "Lu, what of the rice exports to the United States? The GMO rice was to be shipped from Shanghai was it not?"

Chow with bowed head, "Chairman Jun, my staff told me two days ago that the United States Department of Commerce had put an embargo on both the rice contract and that of the freedom bars."

Chairman Jun, in the voice reserved for the mother about to place the sleeping child on its bed, says, "Are you suggesting that there has been a leak of information or that our communications have been infiltrated or compromised?"

Chow, pulling himself even smaller than his normal diminutive size quietly answered, "It appears that there has been an infiltration of communications or traitorous leak that may have alerted the United States of the lethal rice products we were shipping to them, most high and honorable Chairman."

With the speed of a surface to air missile, the Chairman raised the pistol in front of him from the table and shot Minister Chow between the downcast eyes. The details of a leak or infiltration would be discovered through the torture of his subordinates. The United States now knows that China had a plan to reintroduce the HVD to its shores.

Chairman Jun continues by addressing Director-General Lim Fang, "You have checked to ensure that this bombing attack was not perpetrated by laowai from any country across the globe?? And I would like to know why Doctor Yīshēng is not present."

General Fang, "Honorable Chairman, as much as I would like to tell you that this was an action by laowai, for which we could declare war, honesty prevents me from such a declaration. We monitor communications from all countries across the globe. This action could not have been planned and executed without our secure monitoring discovering such a complex plan. The communications breach was much too sophisticated to have been performed by the Americans. This breach was integral in the ability to perform the effectiveness of the bombings, and its superior execution demonstrates that this plan was devised by the superior intellect of Chinese entities.

And Doctor Yīshēng has not been able to be reached. Our intelligence shows him departing his home in Dongguan, two days ago, and being driven to the airport where he was flown to Beijing by private jet. He arrived in Beijing at 4:30, and the jet departed at 5:04. We have no information about the plane other than the flight path to Hong Kong, but it did not arrive."

Chairman Jun, "The two Americans must be dispatched if they were not on the missing plane. I can see plainly that if this action was taken by Chinese nationals, it has been facilitated by traitors within the circle of my trust. Traitors who would destroy the dragon of power that is the state of China. Is it your suggestion, that the failure which allowed this action against our beloved red state falls on that of the Ministry of Communications?"

General Fang bowed his head because he knew that he was about to save his own life as he declared, "Most high and honorable Chairman, the failure does indeed sit at the feet of the weak and lowly Minister of Communications, Li

Ying."

Chairman Jun looked at his military aide, Ying Wei, and slowly nodded. This was the only signal the aide needed. He was required to leave the room, locate, and kill his uncle who has been the Director of Communications. Ying also knew that the next order would be to arrest and transfer to political camps, the remainder of his Uncle's family. He will also locate the Americans to prove his loyalty to the Chairman and thereby save his own life from the stain of his uncle.

Director Cheng who has been silently unobtrusive during these communications has sweat profusely through his clothing but he will wet his undergarments as soon as he exits the room with his life which was saved by the condemnation of the Ministry of Communications.

The Chairman no longer needed to contact Vice President Hoge. This atrocity, happening within his realm, has proven that the century-long plan for China to rule the world would not happen in the lifetime of, or under the rule of, Chairman Jun. He must make a plan now, to remove the target from his own back and find a way to save the lives of his family as well as himself.

DELPHI AND HUAN

Now that the mission was complete Art could turn his intentions back onto the two traitors still in China. He would exact revenge for the lies they told. He would exact revenge for the millions they were party to killing. And, he would exact revenge for the pointless deaths of Terry Angel and Dr. Hampton.

Da had people keeping tabs on both Chuck Delphi and Stephanie Wolff – Art knew exactly where to find them. His first order of business would be to dispatch good ole Chuck, so he armed himself for the task and headed out.

* * *

Mr. Daddy Dickey (a.k.a. Chuck Delphi)

Dickey was a captive in a special kind of 'comfort service' establishment. The place was in a very industrialized area south of downtown Beijing. For such a large and vibrant city it was a surprise that one could find a slum, but there is was, cramped, noisy, and smelly.

The building was nondescript with no entrance on the street out front. Art had to walk a short distance in an alleyway to find the door. Outside stood a very large

Chinese man who looked to be twice Art's size. Art simply reached inside his sport coat, slowly, and extracted a gold coin. As he handed the coin to the bouncer the large man opened the door.

Inside the room was smoky. Art could smell the strong odor of marijuana as he stepped up to the bar. He flashed a picture of Delphi to the bartender who said, "Bon bon," while nodding in the direction of a door at the end of the bar. Art asked, "Laowai?" The bartender only nodded yes.

Art walked to the door and knocked. A small Asian woman opened the door and stood in the doorway. Art again said, "Bon bon," and flashed the picture. Because Art looked American, she replied in her best English, "Last door on left, twenty U.S. dollars." Art removed a U.S. $20.00 bill from his pocket and handed it to the woman before walking past her to the room. He opened the door without knocking and stepped in. Art had smelled a lot of bad things in his life, but the stench in the room almost overwhelmed him. In the dim light of the single bulb, he saw a naked white male sleeping on his back. From the arm closest to him, Art could see numerous bruises from the many injections that man had been given. *Heroin*, he thought as it was almost free in these establishments. There was no doubt that this was the man formerly known as Chuck Delphi.

"Bon bon," Art said softly. Without opening his eyes the man rolled off the puke and blood-stained sheets and then crawled back onto the bed presenting his backside to Art. Something the man now knew as an almost involuntary response. He was defeated and submitting to the power of the drugs and torture he'd been given.

Art reached around his back and withdrew a .45 caliber semi-automatic handgun from the holster in his waistband. He had two, as he was not planning on using a silencer and would undoubtedly need the second to make his exit. He pointed the weapon at the back of the man's head and paused. *He's in hell now where he belongs. Killing him would be merciful.* After a minute or so, Art holstered his weapon and left Bon Bon to die there in his own vomit and blood.

* * *

Huan (a.k.a. Stephanie Wolff)

Art verified through his contact in Taipei that Huan was in a similar, but worse situation. While Bon Bon was barely aware of his situation and completely broken, Huan was not. No, Huan was well aware of her predicament. She was being held in a Taiwanese brothel in the deepest darkest part of the Taipei Red Light District. Her captors kept her minimally drugged, just enough to have some effect and weaken her spirit a bit – customers wanted to hear her screams. They fed her rice and water only – she had lost 11 pounds in only a week and yet retained much of her stunning figure - save for the bruises, welts, and cuts. The Asian men that visited her would pay large sums of money for their pleasure with the white woman.

Her fate was sealed as they would continue to abuse her until she was no longer novel to the cruel clientele. She would remain chained to her pole, beaten and repeatedly raped. When her usefulness was gone, and if she were lucky she'd be dumped far out to sea, still alive, but her end would be quicker. If she was not lucky - her end would be much worse.

EPILOG – ART DAMONE

Sitting in the hotel in Beijing, Art was thinking about his parents and his past. He had no memories of his mother - she had been killed before Art had learned to walk. Raised in military schools, he had no choice to be in any career other than some branch of military service. His father was absent a lot, but there seemed to be an abundance of male role models who were forever focused on his extracurricular paths in martial arts, marksmanship, and munitions.

It wasn't until Art had spent several years performing special operations in the Army that he was informed that his father had been killed in what appeared to be an act of terrorism. When he went to the home that had been his primary residence, he discovered many previously unknown truths about his father, who had been a black operations contractor for the United States government until his identity had been compromised. He had been tortured in the stables of the large home. Art spent more than six months searching the house for some clue that could reveal the possible reason for the death of his father.

All things became clear when he discovered the secret

room within the home. He located the many passports and identities that his father had used for his missions, and diaries of the operations, including the targets and reasons. And he located letters to Art that his father had never sent. His father had been a patriot in every sense of the word, following exactly the requirements of the missions. There were bank accounts in countries around the world containing millions of dollars that could not be accessed by the IRS of the United States, in addition to untold amounts of currency. None of this mattered to Art. His father had left properties and insurance policies to ensure that Art would never need to work a day in his life, but some letters implored Art to forever be loyal to his country because no country in the world offered the freedom of the United States.

His father had expected the attack - he provided one of the names of the Chinese agent who was contracted to kill him. This agent had made attempts against his father for years which was the reason Art had been kept hidden away in military schools and tutored so stridently in the arts of self-protection. The letters from his father were filled with prayers for Art's safety and the admission that his mother had been killed as she protected Art in one of the attacks early in his life.

Soo Lin was a kindred spirit in the political action which caused the loss of her family as well. Perhaps this completed mission may have served to vindicate her loss. Maybe she would be willing to join with him, Goose and LMC to find the murderer of his parents. Art was thinking, *I'm already in China, so why not do a little digging with Soo's help?*

Just then, there was a knock at the hotel room door and a female voice called out from the other side, "Housekeeping." Goose was sitting on the sofa, next to MSA-LMC, and immediately analyzed the voice to ascertain a possible threat level and report to Art. Then, One blink. If Goose could smile, he would have.

A NOTE TO MY READERS ABOUT THE DECOMMISSIONED TRILOGY

The prophetic behavior of the fictional virus in the Decommissioned trilogy has not been edited to reflect the behavior of the 2020 Covid-19 Novel Corona Virus.

At the time Decommissioned was written, in late 2017, there was no real-world Covid-19 pandemic. Though the Decommissioned Trilogy is about a fictional virus, it is different in some ways, from the present worldwide pandemic. The similarities, parallels, and possibilities continue to be staggering......

OTHER BOOKS BY
MARYELLEN HUNTER

<u>DECOMMISSIONED</u>

Book one in the Decommissioned trilogy and the prequel to SAVIOR UNIT.

In Decommissioned Josh and Beth stumble upon the partially decommissioned Medical Services Android (later affectionately named "Goose" – as in golden goose) and work to recommission it. In the process they discover its mission: "MUST SAVE MANKIND" and the reason behind it.

Hunted by the FBI they encounter other individuals who are also discovering the truth to the increasing number of deaths related to a vaccine. As these individual heroes coalesce, the SAVIOR UNIT is formed. Their mission will be to expose the truth and the perpetrators and stop the genocide being wrought on the citizens of the United States.

SAVIOR UNIT
THE SEQUEL TO DECOMMISSIONED

Clearcut was a planned distribution of a biological weapon to radically reduce large numbers of the population within select target groups while saving those contributors to the tax system and specific political voting blocks. The launch of Clearcut returned reports of extraordinary success. The number of deaths was staggering and DComm Group was pleased.

There are some, however, not part of DComm, who know the truth of Project Clearcut. This small team is committed to finding a way to stop Project Clearcut. Their goal is to save the population of the United States and remove the corruption existing in the present administration. They worked undercover, risking their lives to collect the proof of the genocide and to recruit an army of patriots intent upon regaining the freedom of the United States. They are Savior Unit...........

IOTAA
(to be published by Fulton Books 2021)

IOTAA is a story of survival, corruption, greed, adversity, adventure, intrigue, competition, and fantasy – wrapped up and tied with a bow of irony.

IOTAA is a story that will never be forgotten!

ZORBECK

A fictional thriller to be on the market early in 2021. Zorbeck arrives on planet Earth by accident. Its feeding process provides its amorphic ability to recreate more of its kind which must be hunted and destroyed before its food supply is exhausted.

ABOUT THE AUTHOR

Maryellen grew up in Toledo Ohio in the 1940s. Reading was a lifetime of books and stories. As early as her elementary school days there were Encyclopedias with their youth books filled with tales from Huckleberry Finn to Little Women. Every Saturday morning, she made the trek to the local library to borrow the maximum number of books allowed. Near the library was a nursing home, so this weekly trip was a double-duty trip of visiting the elderly of the facility. Reading to the residents, singing songs with and for them, and listening to their tales of their own life experiences was a joy to her.

She was inspired by the thrilling stories by Edgar Allan Poe. The Mask of the Red Death and Telltale Heart were stories to be read many times and still sixty years later hold a special place on the bookshelf. Her love of poetry compelled her to memorize Poe's The Raven and William Ernest Henley's Invictus.

Throughout all the reading, she wrote volumes of letters and prose with no thought of publishing any of them, it was just important to put words on paper.

Her writing style is uniquely designed to allow her audience to envision each character within their imaginations. She creates diversity within her heroes and villains and strives to provide the opportunity for you to share your perceptions of each character.

Facebook:

https://www.facebook.com/maryellen.hunter.1690

https://www.facebook.com/Maryellen-Hunter-Author-Page-106094434607982